The

Gills Creek

Five

The

Gills Creek

Five

A Play

Greg M. Dodd

HARVEST
CHRONICLES

Copyright © 2023 Greg M. Dodd
All rights reserved.
Published by Harvest Chronicles, an imprint of Rolos Tuesday Publishing.
www.gregmdodd.com

ISBN-13: 978-0-9915332-9-9 Paperback, Second Edition
Rolos Tuesday Publishing, Columbia, SC
Printed in the United States of America

"With mirth and laughter, let old wrinkles come."

– William Shakespeare, *The Merchant of Venice*

PREFACE

Since first publishing *A Seed for the Harvest* in May of 2014, I've experienced, on several occasions, what any author should consider a gift: conversations with readers of my work. For the author, the exchange is often like watching someone walk across a canyon on a tightrope in high winds. He waits with dreadful anticipation while enjoying the thrill of the moment, just the same. And while he takes great pleasure in receiving such informal, personal feedback, the vast silence from remaining unknown readers leaves him to wonder about unexpressed, perhaps more critical opinions.

After offering discounted book club pricing for *A Seed for the Harvest* in July of last year, I began to imagine how those group discussions might possibly go. Immediately clear was the fact that without the author's fragile ego hovering over the discourse, honest opinions would find freedom of expression. And any literary discussion worthy of someone's evening away from home must have basic elements of conflict, humor and resolution. Otherwise, the quality of the gathering is measured simply by the age of the doughnuts and the warmth of the coffee. It was from these imagined meetings that the idea for *The Gills Creek Five* came.

D. H. Lawrence once said, "The proper function of the critic is to save the tale from the artist who created it." And so it was with my illusory book club critics. The play and its characters, once conceived, seemed to follow a path having little to do with my original intent, in effect, saving the tale from the author who created it.

As you read, my hope is that you will be entertained, challenged and inspired. And for readers of *A Seed for the Harvest*, please accept this story as my gift to you.

Greg M. Dodd
Columbia, SC 2017

CONTENTS

Characters

DANE, group leader
SAM
RETT
EMILE
MARTIN
JUDITH

Scene

A church classroom in Columbia, South Carolina

Time

Wednesday night at 6:30

ACT ONE

Scene One

An empty, medium-sized classroom with two doors – one on each side – and two windows overlooking the Gills Creek Church parking lot. Twelve folding chairs dot the floor in no particular pattern. SAM *enters the room. After a brief study and count of chairs, he goes about shifting each one until they form a perfect u-shape with ninety-degree corners. Satisfied with his arrangement, he sits down in a chair at the top of the formation. After a minute of waiting alone, tapping his foot and humming, he stands and leaves the room.*

DANE *enters through the other door carrying a box full of books. After setting the box down on a table just inside the door, he evaluates the angular arrangement of chairs, shakes his head and begins shifting each one until they form a smooth, arching, semi-circle facing one lone chair.*

SAM *re-enters the room. Seeing an unfamiliar face and a different configuration of chairs than the one he had just left, he steps back out into the hallway to check the room number, then re-enters.*

DANE: [*offers his hand*] Hello. Welcome, I'm Dane.
SAM: Ah, yes. Hello. [*extends his hand and strides toward* DANE, *shakes* DANE's *hand up and down with deliberately firm pumps*]
DANE: And your name?
SAM: [*still shaking* DANE's *hand*] Oh, right. Sam. I'm Sam.

13

DANE: [*frees his hand from* SAM's *grip*] Nice to meet you, Sam. Please, have a seat.

SAM: [*takes a moment to study the chairs*] Uh....

DANE: Anywhere is fine.

SAM: [*decides on a particular chair*] Ah, yes. Thank you. [*sits down*]

DANE: [*takes a seat in the chair facing the others*] I gather from your accent that you're from England.

SAM: Yes.

DANE: [*smiles*] You didn't come all the way from London just for this, did you? [*chuckles*]

SAM: No, from my office, actually. It's not far from here. About a mile in that direction, I believe. [*points over* DANE's *head*]

    [*A slight pause*]

DANE: [*clears his throat and resets himself*] So...how did you hear about the small group, Sam?

SAM: Well, strange thing, that.

DANE: Oh, really? How so?

SAM: Yes, well, I was examining a patient one day last week, a cat. Bad paw, you know. And—

DANE: You're a vet?

SAM: Right. I'm a veterinarian. Small animals, mostly. [*sighs*] Farm animals just weren't for me, I'm afraid. I tried to help an expectant horse deliver a foal once but felt I was mostly just getting in the way. So, I decided to stick with the smaller household varieties. Cats, dogs, rabbits and the like. If I had to say, I think I'm partial to dogs. They just seem more appreciative than cats. Or rabbits, for that matter.

    [*A pause*]

DANE: [*raises his eyebrows*] And you heard about our study, how?

SAM: Hmm? Oh, yes...where was I?

DANE: You were looking at a cat's paw.

SAM: Yes, of course. I was looking at a cat's paw. [*pauses and frowns*]

DANE: [*with a mixture of amusement and frustration*] And the study group....

SAM: Ah, right, right. Well, as I said, I was looking at a cat's paw – I think it may have been infected. You know, cats can get into the worst of things. Garbage, rose bushes, car engines. It's hard to say how the little lass hurt herself.

DANE: [*with resignation*] Mmhmm.

SAM: Dogs may eat garbage, but they rarely climb into it. Lots of things in a dumpster to nick a curious feline's paw. [*chuckles slightly*] Not to mention the bacteria. [*becomes conscious of* DANE's *blank stare*] Oh, right. The study. Yes. So, I was giving her paw the once-over and its owner asked me where I went to church. Which I thought was a rather strange thing to ask a veterinarian.

DANE: Why is that strange, Sam?

SAM: Well, it had nothing to do with the cat, you see? Then she told me about this church and how I should go to it.

DANE: And you did?

SAM: [*shakes his head affirmatively*] Yes, this past Sunday morning.

DANE: And that's how you found out about the study?

SAM: Yes. I sat next to a very pleasant man – a doctor of some sort – who seemed to be quite the authority on a number of topics. Church related, mostly. He told me I needed to come to a new men's study group, meeting on Wednesday nights here at the church. He didn't say what the study was about, just that I needed to go. [*looks inquisitively at* DANE]

DANE: Do you remember his name?

SAM: Hmm. It was a rather odd name. So, you'd think I'd remember. [*holds his chin in thought*] Or perhaps that's why it escapes me.

[RETT *appears in the doorway holding a Starbucks coffee cup in his hand.*]

RETT: Samuel! You came!

DANE: [*to himself*] I should have known.

RETT: Hey, Dane!

DANE: Rett.

SAM: [*stands*] Hello…Doctor, was it?

RETT: [*shakes* SAM's *hand*] Yes, Dr. Ovaretton T. McCasguill. Good to see you again, Samuel. I'm glad you decided to join our little l'étude des homes.

[DANE *chuckles to himself.*]

[RETT *and* SAM *take their seats.*]

DANE: Rett, my French dates back to high school, but I think you just said we're going to be studying men.

RETT: Well, I'm sure he knew what I meant. Right, Samuel?

SAM: Actually, it's–

RETT: Why, I can spot a man of high culture a mile away. [*slaps* SAM *on the shoulder*] Being one myself, that is.

DANE: [*rolls his eyes*] Well, for the sake of us common folk, what do you say we just stick to English? I'm sure you can sound just as important without butchering the French language.

RETT: [*ignores* DANE] Samuel, how's that cat you were telling me about, Sunday?

SAM: Ah, infected paw, I'm afraid. And I go by–

RETT: Hmm. Sorry to hear that. [*turns to* DANE] Dane, ol' Samuel is here vis-a-vis my invitation this past Sunday in worship. We sat next to each other and – knowing you were leading us – I assured him he needed to be here.

DANE: Yeah, he was just telling me about that. So, what's been going on with you lately, Rett? Are you still in the job market, or have you settled into something?

RETT: Oh, I'm evaluating [*crosses his legs*] several viable prospects at the moment, Dane.

DANE: [*smirks*] I'm sure you are.

RETT: It's not clear, though, at the present time, which opportunity presents the more promising path for someone of my varied skills and abilities. But I've sent my curriculum vitae to several would be suitors and trust that I'll hear something soon.

DANE: Mmhmm.

RETT: But, until then, I'll just keep listening for the Lord's direction and go where he leads me. Life's a journey, Dane. And I invite you and Samuel to come along with me.

SAM: Uh, I'm sorry, where is it that we're going?

RETT: I meant a journey in the metaphorical sense, Samuel. A search for life's higher calling, as it were. Are you with me?

SAM: Uh....

[EMILE *enters, stopping in the doorway.*]

EMILE: Hey. Is this the men's thing?

DANE: [*stands*] I guess you could call it that. Come on in. I'm Dane.

EMILE: [*moves into the room*] Cool. I'm Emile. [*finds himself in the middle of the semi-circle as he shakes* DANE's *hand*]

DANE: Emile, this is Sam and Rett.

RETT: [*stands and shakes* EMILE's *hand*] Dr. Ovaretton T. McCasguill, Emile. Pleasure to make your acquaintance.

SAM: [*stands*] Hello, Emile. I'm Sam.

[EMILE *shakes* SAM's *hand, and all four men sit down.*]

DANE: Emile, are you new to Gills Creek? I don't think I've seen you around, before.

EMILE: What do you mean?

DANE: Um…I just haven't seen you, before, so—

EMILE: So, you're basically saying that you couldn't possibly miss seeing a big, fat guy like me walking around, right?

DANE: Oh. No, I—

EMILE: [*puts up his hand*] It's OK, dude. I'm a big guy; I know that. But no, I'm not new. I've been coming here a couple months.

DANE: Well, Emile, I'm sorry. I didn't mean to offend you.

EMILE: No, forget it, man. [*shakes his head*] I shouldn't have gone there. I'm just a little sensitive about my weight, is all.

RETT: Emile, I believe it's what's inside a man that matters, not any external façade we may cast about for others to see. It's the size of the heart that measures a man.

EMILE: Yeah, well…whatever. [*pauses, then looks at* RETT] Ovaretton…hey, aren't you that dude who taught a Wednesday night class, last month? I remember seeing your name in the paper thing they hand out in church.

RETT: The bulletin. Yes, Emile, that was me. [*smiles and leans back in his chair*] I asked the church if I could teach a class on evangelism, and they were happy to oblige. As a former pastor, I wanted to offer my insight and experience to the cause of spreading the Gospel. You should have joined us.

EMILE: Yeah. So, do a lot of people show up for something like that?

RETT: Well, it's not the size of the class that counts. It's how the Lord can use those who do attend.

DANE: So, how many did you have, Rett?

RETT: [*uncrosses his legs and clears his throat*] Well, Dane, I had six sign-up…but only two men came.

DANE: Two?

RETT: [*nods*] For the first week, anyway. Then one of the gentlemen found out he was deathly allergic to bee stings, so he stopped coming.

SAM: Um, why would that lead him to stop attending your class?

RETT: He was stung by a bee.

SAM: Oh, yes. That would do it, I suppose.

RETT: So, for the last three weeks it was just me and one person. But, you know, if that one man can lead someone else to Christ, then it was well worth my time.

DANE: Who was it? Do you remember his name?

RETT: Walter somebody. He didn't register for the class, but I remember that from his nametag. Older gentleman, very quiet. But I'm always thankful for a good listener, Dane. I take it as a personal compliment and a sign of appreciation for all the hard work I put into my lessons. [*smiles with satisfaction*]

DANE: You know Walter's deaf, don't you?

RETT: He's what?

DANE: He's deaf.

RETT: Are you sure?

DANE: Yep. He just likes to find somewhere to hang out on Wednesday nights while his wife is in choir practice.

RETT: Oh. [*frowns in thought*] Well…that might explain a few things, I guess.

DANE: I thought it might.

[MARTIN *enters, pauses just inside the door, appearing a bit unsteady.*]

MARTIN: Hello, gents! Am I in the right place?

DANE: Sure, come on in. We were just about to get started.

[MARTIN *drifts into the room and plops down heavily on a chair between* EMILE *and* SAM. SAM *sniffs the air in* MARTIN's *direction as* MARTIN *settles in next to him.*]

DANE: I'm Dane and–

MARTIN: [*holds up his index finger*] Hold that thought. I need proof that I'm here. [*takes out his iPhone, puts his arm around a confused* SAM *and takes a selfie*] That's a good man. Let me just send this to the wife. [*types on his phone with both thumbs, then returns the phone to his pocket*] OK. Now, please continue.

DANE: We were just doing introductions. I'm Dane. What's your name?

MARTIN: Oh, right, of course. [*nods to* SAM] I love this part. I'll go first. [*stands*] Hello. I'm Martin. And I'm an alcoholic. [*giggles to himself as he sits and elbows* SAM]

SAM: [*glances around, a bit unsure*] Right. I guess I'm next, then. [*stands*] Hello. I'm Sam. And I'm a veterinarian.

[MARTIN *bursts out laughing.*]

DANE: No, Sam, I think Martin's in the wrong place.

MARTIN: What? You mean I've walked into a group for Veterinarians Anonymous? [*keeps laughing*]

DANE: I take it you were looking for the Alcoholics Anonymous meeting.

MARTIN: This isn't AA? [*looks around*] You fellows sure look like you could all use a drink. [*snickers*]

DANE: This is a men's study group. AA meets in the gym. It's just down the hall to the left.

MARTIN: [*appears serious*] A men's study group, hmm? I guess that's close enough. Mind if I hide out here for a bit?

DANE: [*glances around at* SAM, RETT *and* EMILE] Well, anyone is welcome, but I don't–

MARTIN: Excellent! I wasn't looking forward to all that preachy twelve-step business, again, anyway. I get it: Don't drink! They should just say that and cut the whole program down to one step and save everyone a lot of time. [*giggles*] But I got myself into a bit of a spot with the wife, you see. So, she forced me – I mean – I promised her to [*makes air quotes with his fingers*] get help. [*giggles*]

RETT: [*leans forward, resting his elbows on his knees*] Martin, I – for one – believe it may be divine providence that led you here, tonight. I can't speak for the rest of us, but the help you need might be found right here in this room.

MARTIN: You have gin?

RETT: No.

MARTIN: Vodka?

RETT: No. I'm referring to the fellowship of Christian brethren, men of faith gathered together to find strength for the journey of life. Proverbs 13:20 says, "Walk with the wise and become wise." I invite you to join us as we seek to store up treasures in heaven.

MARTIN: So…no gin, huh?

DANE: Rett, why don't you help Martin find the AA meeting in the gym? I think that's where he needs to be.

MARTIN: No, no, I'm in. I'm in. What he just said: brethren, life, treasure…or something like that. I'm in.

DANE: Well, I don't think–

RETT: Welcome to the group, Martin!

[DANE *casts an irritated glare at* RETT.]

21

MARTIN: [*imitating Elvis Presley*] Why, thank you. Thank you, very much. [*giggles*] So, what are we studying here in our very own men's study group?

[*A slight pause*]

DANE: [*sighs*] I guess that's a good segue to an introduction.

MARTIN: Wonderful! See? I'm helping, already.

DANE: Yeah. Anyway, we're going to be reading a novel from a local Christian author, whom I met in a coffee shop a few months ago.

RETT: Starbucks? [*holds up his cup*]

DANE: No. I wouldn't be caught dead in a Starbucks.

RETT: Why? You used to love good coffee back in the day.

DANE: I still do. And that's why I wouldn't be caught dead in a Starbucks.

RETT: But everybody likes Starbucks, Dane. It's good coffee.

DANE: You've obviously never tasted a good cup of coffee.

RETT: Well, I like it. It has a certain je ne sais quoi.

DANE: [*moans*] Stop with the French, already. When did all that start, anyway?

RETT: Dane, you can't live in Louisiana and not become acclimated to the French language to some degree. In fact, my favorite Starbucks barista in Brouillette taught me most of what I know.

DANE: Starbucks doesn't have baristas, Rett; they have high school students. Besides, do you even know where Starbucks gets their beans from? Or where and how they're roasted?

RETT: For heaven sakes, Dane, it's just coffee. It's hot water with stuff in it.

DANE: OK, come with me to the Lost Bean, sometime, and I'll teach you how to enjoy real coffee. Not that corporate swill you get at Starbucks.

EMILE: Um, not to interrupt your little coffee snob debate or anything, but you were about to tell us what we'll be studying.

DANE: Oh, I'm sorry about that, Emile. [*resets himself*] Coffee is just a little passion of mine. Anyway, yes, the title of the book is *A Seed for the Harvest*. Here, I brought your copies. [*stands, walks to the table near the door, retrieves four books from the box and hands a copy to* SAM, RETT *and* EMILE]

DANE: Martin, I have one here for you, if you're serious about joining us. It's ten dollars.

MARTIN: Oh, I'm fresh out of cash at the moment.

DANE: It's OK. You can pay me if you come back next week. If not, just keep it. [*hands a book to* MARTIN]

MARTIN: [*feels the weight of the book in his hands*] It's awfully heavy.

DANE: We'll read it over the next eight weeks and discuss what we've read each week.

MARTIN: Well, if it's not worth reading, I could always use it as a weapon to fend off the neighbor's dog. [*swings the book back and forth*] Mangy fleabag.

SAM: It pays to be careful with that, you know.

MARTIN: With what? The book? I don't think I'll break it.

SAM: [*shakes his head*] No, the mange. You mustn't get too close to your neighbor's dog. You wouldn't want to get scabies.

MARTIN: [*looks curiously at* SAM] No, I guess not. Might be hard to explain to the wife. [*giggles to himself*]

SAM: It's a mite infestation. Nasty little creatures, mites. My assistant caught them once from a hamster. Ugliest thing you've ever seen.

MARTIN: [*grins*] Your assistant?

SAM: No, the hamster. Of course, my assistant is rather unattractive herself, I suppose. Particularly when her hair began falling out in spots. Almost scratched herself out of a job, poor thing. Couldn't have her around the animals, you know. Very contagious.

[*A pause*]

DANE: OK, so—

SAM: Tell your neighbor to bring the dog to see me. I have a good treatment for mites.

MARTIN: Let me guess: You'll bore them to death. [*snickers*]

SAM: [*unfazed*] No, a topical cream, actually. Works very well.

DANE: So, as I was saying, guys – if I may continue – that I met the author down at the Lost Bean. That's how I found out about the book. He was doing character research for a play he's writing and asked to interview me. Being a bit of a writer myself, I was immediately intrigued. Although, after a few questions, I realized he was using his character research as a way to find witnessing opportunities with strangers.

RETT: Hmm. That's pretty clever.

DANE: I thought so.

EMILE: Sounds kinda sneaky to me. [*looks at* SAM] Wouldn't you say so, Sam?

SAM: I'm not sure I follow.

MARTIN: He's saying the guy was posing as a writer but actually pushing Jesus on unsuspecting caffeine addicts.

SAM: Oh. Uh....

DANE: First of all, he wasn't posing as a writer, Martin; he is a writer. And I assure you, there was nothing subversive about what he was doing. He was simply looking to engage people in faith conversations. And, as it happens, that's what his book is about. And I thought it would make a great study topic for our group.

RETT: Have you read it, Dane?

DANE: I have, actually. And I really enjoyed it. It does have a bit of a twisted ending, so be ready for that.

RETT: [*looks at the book in his hands*] How much would you like us to read for next week?

DANE: I stuck a reading plan in each of your books that will guide you each week.

EMILE: [*fans the pages of the book*] Dude, this book has 455 pages in it. And no pictures. That's a lot of reading. Couldn't we do something, like, anything by Ray Bradbury?

DANE: Ray Bradbury wrote short stories.

EMILE: That's kinda my point.

DANE: I promise, Emile, it's a quick read with a good message. I knocked it out on my own in two weeks.

MARTIN: You must have skipped every other word.

DANE: Guys, trust me. You'll like it.

EMILE: [*shrugs as he flips through the book*] If you say so.

DANE: OK, since we're going to be together for a few weeks, why don't we go around the room and tell a little about ourselves.

[MARTIN *groans.*]

DANE: I'll start. As I said, my name is Dane. I'm an eighth grade English literature teacher.

RETT: Teacher and author. Don't sell yourself short, Dane.

DANE: [*to the rest of the group*] I'm not an author. I've just written a manuscript for my first novel, that's all. But I'm hoping to see it published.

RETT: [*holds the book up*] Dane, if this local nobody can self-publish a book like this, you can, too. You need to go for it. Tu peux le faire!

25

DANE: Whatever that means. I'll just stick to the traditional publishing route, Rett, thank you. My agent is doing the best she can.

RETT: You told me she calls you Dave whenever you call her on the phone.

MARTIN: [*giggles*] Ouch.

DANE: That's only happened a few times. She has a lot of clients; it's an honest mistake. Besides, last week she got my manuscript in front of a new publisher. And it sounds very promising.

EMILE: What's your book about, man?

DANE: Well, [*appears thoughtful*] it's somewhat autobiographical, I suppose. But it's mostly fiction. It's—

MARTIN: Not to be rude, although I suppose I am, but what is there about an eighth grade English lit teacher's life that would be worthy of a memoir? [*tries not to laugh*]

DANE: [*casts a glare at* MARTIN] Hence, the need for fiction.

MARTIN: Ah, spruced your story up a bit, eh? So, in the book, are you a *tenth* grade English lit teacher? [*giggles*]

EMILE: Dude, not cool.

DANE: Guys, can we get back on topic, please? Martin, you're welcome to stay, but please—

MARTIN: Sorry, sorry. I'll be quiet. I promise. I'll just sit right here and listen. No more out of me. I won't say a word.

DANE: You can talk, but just remember, we're here to learn and encourage one another.

MARTIN: Roger that. Go ahead, Dave.

[DANE *looks at* MARTIN *and sighs.*]

[MARTIN *returns a grin.*]

EMILE: [*to* DANE] You want me to carry him down to the AA meeting in the gym?

DANE: No, Emile, he's fine. Anyway…I teach English literature and, yes, I like to write, as well. I love coffee, and I'm divorced. No kids. That's me in a nutshell.

MARTIN: So, how long is your book, then? Maybe he'd rather read it, instead. [*gestures toward* EMILE]

EMILE: [*raises a cautionary eyebrow at* MARTIN *and points in the direction of the gym*] Dude?

DANE: Emile, it's all right. Let's move on. Rett, how about you?

RETT: Ah, well. My name is Dr. Ovaretton T. McCasguill. And I'm the former Pastor of Dead Oak Baptist Church in Brouillette, Louisiana, where I served the Lord for six years, then was called back to my birth state of South Carolina to begin a new journey, a new chapter, as it were, details about which I'm patiently waiting for God to reveal to me. Oh, and I have three children.

DANE: I thought you said four, Rett.

RETT: [*chuckles at himself*] Thank you, Dane. I got so used to saying three it became a habit. But, yes, I have four children, all girls. The youngest is just six months.

EMILE: So, like, [*points at* RETT *and* DANE] you two guys know each other?

DANE: We were in college together twenty years ago. We haven't seen each other since then, until Rett moved back from Louisiana.

RETT: And Dane hasn't changed a bit since I knew him back in the day.

DANE: You have, Rett.

RETT: Well, I've been on the Potter's wheel, so to speak, Dane. God has molded me into what you see here today. All glory goes to him.

MARTIN: Why do I suddenly feel so discouraged?

DANE: [*holds back a slight smirk*] Sam, what about you?

SAM: Oh, uh....

DANE: Just tell us a little about yourself.

SAM: Oh, right. Well. I'm a veterinarian.

DANE: I think we got that part. Is there anything else you'd like to share?

SAM: Such as?

DANE: Do you have any hobbies? Are you married, single? Do you have any pets?

SAM: Uh, well...I am single. And, no, I have no pets.

EMILE: You're a vet, and you don't have a pet? How is that possible?

SAM: Well, I suppose my patients are my pets.

EMILE: No, come on, man. A vet's gotta have a pet. I think it's the law or something.

SAM: Oh, uh....

MARTIN: Forget about pets. How about a girlfriend?

SAM: [shakes his head] No, I'm afraid I haven't much luck in the field of romance. It seems I never know what to say around women.

MARTIN: Hmm, that could be a problem.

SAM: Yes, quite. I'm always afraid I'll say something they won't like, you see. The result of which is that I never really say much at all. And they don't seem to like that, either.

MARTIN: I think I can be of help to you in that category, my friend.

SAM: That would be very kind of you, Martin. What would you suggest?

MARTIN: Well, first, you get a bottle of gin and–

DANE: Thank you, Martin. That's enough.

MARTIN: Just trying to help our two-legged friend, here. [pats SAM on the head] You said be encouraging.

DANE: [shakes his head at MARTIN] Emile, how about you?

EMILE: Yeah, sure. So, I'm Emile. [*waves his hand*] I'm twenty-four and…I live with my mom. Actually, she lives with me.

RETT: What kind of work do you do, Emile?

EMILE: Oh, I do, you know, volunteer and charity stuff, mostly.

MARTIN: We call that being unemployed.

EMILE: I stay busy, dude. I just don't have a job-job, like most people.

DANE: Are you currently looking for work, Emile? Because the church has people who could–

EMILE: No, I'm good. Thanks. But besides that, I'm not married, and I like to play video games and tabletop fantasy role-play games, like HeroQuest and Feng Shui.

MARTIN: Hence, why he's not married.

EMILE: [*slightly irritated*] Let's hear about your life, dude. Doesn't sound all that great to me, so far.

MARTIN: All right. Fair enough, my round friend. [*pats EMILE on the knee*] Would anyone else like to hear my story?

DANE: By all means. It's why we're here.

MARTIN: Ah, a captive audience just for me. [*rubs his hands together*] Perfect. Well, here goes…I've been married to my sweet bride, Judith, for over [*counts in his head*] five years now, or something like that. And, yes, as our portly charity-worker said–

EMILE: Seriously?

MARTIN: –things could be better. I admit that. But my – I mean our – marital problems, you see, aren't my fault. [*waves his index finger*] Not at all. This isn't a case of "it's not you, it's me." It really is her. She's the problem. She won't do anything with me, you see? "Let's go away for a weekend," I say. "No, Martin, I'm too busy around

29

the house," she says. "Let's make love in the garage," I say. "No Martin, I have too much work to do."

EMILE: Dude, the garage?

MARTIN: It's always "No, Martin" this and "No, Martin" that. I know I could make her happy, if she'd only let me. But she'd rather be miserable. She chooses to be miserable. It's really not my doing.

DANE: Martin, you came here tonight looking for an AA meeting. You don't think your drinking has something to do with how your wife treats you?

MARTIN: Ah, the writer, the English lit teacher, of all people, falls for the obvious plot line: Sweet, loving wife endures awful marriage to raging alcoholic. Is that it? Surely, you're more creative than that, Dave. The best stories always have a twist, don't they? You should know that. I tell you what, you want some character research for your next novel? Let me tell you about my wife. My wife...my wife just doesn't love me, you see? But that's OK. I can't really fault her for that. I'm a stinking librarian's assistant at the county library. She doesn't go around bragging about her husband's career, I can tell you that. She's ashamed of me. All right, fine. But the problem is that she won't let me love her. That's all I want to do. I just want to make her happy. Does that make me so rotten? Am I so awful as all that? And so what if I drink? A man has to feel good, somehow, doesn't he? A man needs to feel like a man, not some emasculated piece of furniture that gets vacuumed around on Saturdays. [*drops his head*] It's her fault for not seeing that.

[*A long pause*]

EMILE: Dude, that's messed up.

MARTIN: [*laughs*] It really is, isn't it?

[DANE *looks at his watch. He and* RETT *exchange glances.*]

RETT: Martin, I told you there's a reason you stumbled in here, tonight. We're here to listen and support each other. And I hope you'll come back next week.

MARTIN: [*sniffs his nose*] Well, my wife expects me to be *somewhere* next Wednesday evening. And given the alternative, I may join you, again…if you'll have me.

RETT: You're welcome here, Martin.

SAM: So, Martin, what do I do after I get the gin?

DANE: He was just kidding about that, Sam.

SAM: Oh.

DANE: Weren't you, Martin?

MARTIN: No, actually–

DANE: OK, guys, I think that's enough for this week. You've got your reading assignments for next time. It's only fifty or sixty pages.

[EMILE *moans.*]

MARTIN: [*to* EMILE] Honestly, what else do you have to do?

EMILE: I don't know, dude. I might do…something. You never know.

MARTIN: Hmm, that sounds exciting. Can I come?

DANE: All right, guys. Read that and we'll discuss it next week. Rett, would you mind closing us in prayer, and we'll call it a night?

RETT: Oui, monsieur.

[DANE *sighs as the group bows their heads to pray.*]

Curtain

ACT ONE

Scene Two

The classroom. DANE *enters and drops his book onto a chair. Appearing somewhat irritated, he moves four chairs into a semi-circle facing one lone chair, then begins to fold the remaining chairs and move them to the side of the room.* RETT *enters, unnoticed by* DANE.

RETT: [*smiles*] Bonjour, mon ami!

DANE: [*glances up to see* RETT, *shakes his head and continues moving chairs*] Hey, Rett. [*stops and turns to look at* RETT] Oh, I'm sorry, should I call you Ovaretton? [*continues folding chairs*]

RETT: [*tosses his book on a chair and begins to help move the chairs against the wall*] "Rett" sounds a little more apropos, coming from you, I suppose.

DANE: [*becomes frustrated as he struggles to fold an uncooperative chair*] Or, maybe I should call you "Dr. McCasguill," hmm?

RETT: [*stops moving chairs and looks at* DANE] Have I done something to offend you, Dane? Because I'm picking up on some sort of weird vibe, here.

DANE: You? Conscious of someone else's vibe? That would be weird.

RETT: Now, see? Something's definitely bothering you.

DANE: [*continues moving chairs with a hint of impatience*] No, no. Nothing's wrong. I suppose I should thank you again for lunch Sunday. You didn't have to pay for both of us, though.

RETT: [*watches* DANE] It was my pleasure. I enjoyed catching up with my old college buddy.

DANE: [*stops and faces* RETT] Rett, honestly, you didn't catch up with me. You didn't ask anything about me. You just gave me an hour-long dissertation on your walk with God, remember?

RETT: [*laughs as he folds a chair and leans it against the wall*] Well, the Lord has given me a long story to tell, hasn't he?

DANE: OK, you know, what? I'm sorry, there *is* something bothering me.

RETT: Ah, I knew it. You see? The old Pastor's insight is never wrong. You can't fool me, Dane.

DANE: I just need to say one thing before the other guys get here.

RETT: Of course, get it off your chest. Confession time.

DANE: [*shakes his head*] Whatever. Look, I get that you found Christ after we knew each other in college and pastored a church for five years—

RETT: Six.

DANE: Fine, six. Whatever. But what are you doing here?

RETT: I'm not sure what you mean.

DANE: Rett, you're so intent on letting everyone know you're *Dr.* Ovaretton T. McCasguill and that you're God's gift to ministry, I'd think you'd have bigger fish to fry than my little small group here.

RETT: Ah...I see.

DANE: See what?

RETT: What's really bothering you.

DANE: And what is that?

RETT: You're worried that I'll take over your group, aren't you?

DANE: This isn't a competition, Rett. We're not back in college.

RETT: Then what are you worried about?

DANE: Look, I've got this whole study planned out, and I know how I want it to go. I know it's not a big group, but I think I can help Sam and Emile grow in their faith. Or get faith. Either one. But it can't be all about you, OK?

RETT: What about Martin?

DANE: Martin? That's another thing. Thank you for encouraging a practicing alcoholic to skip AA, lie to his wife about it and join our group.

RETT: Well, he seemed like he needed someone to talk to.

DANE: AA, Rett! He was going to AA. That's where he needs to be. But, no, you have to tell him that God wants him in here.

RETT: How do you know he doesn't?

DANE: Fine, I don't. But if he does come back this week, you're going to babysit him, not me. He's your responsibility.

RETT: [shakes his head] You're still just as tightly wound as you used to be, aren't you, Dane? You really need to lighten up.

[SAM appears in the doorway, unnoticed by RETT and DANE.]

DANE: Look, I'm sorry to get bent out of shape about all this. But can you just go along with everything, or do you have to be the center of attention, like always?

[SAM enters cautiously.]

SAM: Hello.

DANE: [a bit startled] Oh, hey, Sam. I didn't see you there. Come on in. [glances at RETT] We were just....

SAM: I'm a bit too early, aren't I? I'll just go back out and—

DANE: No, please, Sam, come on in. Have a seat.

RETT: Hello, Samuel. How was your week?

SAM: Hello, Doctor.

RETT: Please, call me Rett. We're all friends, here. Right, Dane?

DANE: One would hope so, yes. [*turns to place the remaining extra chair against the wall*]

SAM: [*to* RETT] I'll strike a bargain with you, Doctor. I'll call you Rett, if you call me Sam.

RETT: I think I can agree to that, Sam. [*takes a seat on the end of the row of four chairs*] So, tell me, did you save any cats this week?

[DANE *turns and shakes his head quickly at* RETT.]

SAM: [*sits down*] As a matter of fact, [DANE *drops his head*] the same cat I told you about last week was in to see me again.

DANE: [*sighs*] Same bad paw? [*sits down in the chair facing the other four chairs*]

SAM: No. Constipated. And my fault, I'm afraid.

RETT: [*chuckles*] A constipated cat? How would you even know?

SAM: Clean litter box. It's a dead giveaway. The medication I prescribed for her paw stopped her right up.

RETT: Oh.

SAM: Very serious condition, constipation.

RETT: What did you do?

[EMILE *enters.*]

SAM: I gave her an enema.

[EMILE *stops.*]

SAM: Cleaned her right out. Happy as she could be after that.

RETT: Yeah, well, who wouldn't be?

EMILE: Uh, guys? What the....

DANE: [*turns to see* EMILE] Hey, Emile. Sam was just telling us another cat story.

EMILE: [*relieved*] Oh, dude.... [*moves into the room and takes a seat on the end of the row next to* SAM] I forgot you were a vet.

SAM: Oh, yes. No change there.

DANE: So, how are you, Emile? Having a good week?

EMILE: Sure, I guess. Anything's better than giving out cat enemas. Dude, that sounds nasty.

SAM: It's actually a very simple procedure. You see, you take warm water and a tube–

DANE: Uh, Sam. That's OK, really.

SAM: Ah, yes. Sorry.

EMILE: [*to* DANE] So, you think that drunk dude is coming back this week?

DANE: Martin? I don't know. We probably shouldn't wait on him.

EMILE: I kinda hope he doesn't. I know that's not a cool churchy-type thing to say, but…the guy has issues, man.

DANE: Well, don't we all?

EMILE: Yeah, but…sex in the garage? I mean, what's that all about?

DANE: Emile, I think we need to make a commitment to each other that what we say in here stays in here.

EMILE: Sure, but…I'm saying it in here. The guy has issues.

RETT: I think what Dane means, Emile, is that we treat each other with respect and don't talk behind each other's backs. Is that right, Dane?

DANE: Yes, thank you, Rett.

EMILE: That's fine. I was just saying.

   [*The sound of* MARTIN *singing can be heard from down the hall.*]

EMILE: Oh, terrific.

MARTIN: [*sings as he enters the room with a slight stagger*] "Oh, I'm sorry I broke your heart, Mother." Evening, gents! [*smiles broadly, opens his arms wide and takes a bow*]

DANE: [*lacking enthusiasm*] Martin. You made it.

MARTIN: Yes, I did! [*crosses the room and plops down in the chair between* SAM *and* RETT] And I even did my homework.

37

All thirteen chapters. Do I get an A, Mr. English lit teacher?

SAM: [*leans toward* EMILE *and whispers*] I could be wrong about this, but I believe Martin may have had a drink before coming.

EMILE: [*loudly*] Dude, whatever gave you that idea?

SAM: [*looks to* DANE] Uh, well....

DANE: Martin, how much did you have to drink before coming here?

MARTIN: [*thoughtfully*] That's a very difficult question to answer, Dave.

DANE: Why is that?

MARTIN: Because I've been drinking for years. [*giggles to himself*]

DANE: OK, how much did you drink tonight?

MARTIN: Are you suggesting that I've over indulged, kind sir?

DANE: That's putting it mildly. Maybe it would be best if you went home. Or to the AA meeting in the gym.

RETT: [*leans forward and speaks in a low voice*] Dane, I know he shouldn't be here like this, but I don't think we can send him away, either. Let's see if he sobers-up a bit while we talk.

MARTIN: [*leans in and whispers*] That's a good idea. Let's do that. [*giggles as he leans back*]

DANE: [*sighs*] Martin, do you think you can behave yourself?

MARTIN: Oh, of course. No worries about me. I'll be a model student. [*aligns his loose neck tie with the buttons on his short-sleeve dress shirt*]

DANE: Well, if you can't, I'm going to call a cab and tell them to take you home to your wife.

MARTIN: [*sits straighter in his chair*] I'll be good. I'll be good. I promise. [*gives* DANE *a salute*]

DANE: All right. Well, I suppose we can get started, then. [*opens the notebook on his lap*] Did everyone read the first thirteen chapters?

MARTIN: [*shoots his hand up in the air*] I did!

DANE: Yes, we know, Martin. How about everyone else?

[*Each of the other three give an affirming nod.*]

DANE: OK, good. So, would anyone like to summarize what we've read, so far?

[RETT *raises his hand and opens his mouth to speak.*]

DANE: Anyone besides Rett?

[RETT *appears befuddled.*]

EMILE: I can take a stab at it.

DANE: OK, Emile, go ahead.

EMILE: Well, this dude, Jon, the main character guy, has this dog, named Elvis, see, but it's not really his dog. It's his daughter Holly's dog. But she's away at college, except for the part when she was a little girl without a mom, but we're not really sure where she is – the mom. And Jon meets this girl named Amy in a beach arcade thing when he was twelve, and then he loses his Bible for a couple weeks, but then he gives Elvis a treat, and he finds it in his car – his Bible, I mean – and then he's all mad about it and stuff, and he cries in front of his Sunday school class. And then he tells-off this Sunday school guy after he runs into an old friend named Brant who he went to a football game with. Dude, did you know there's a cuss word in this book?

MARTIN: [*slaps his forehead*] Holy, crap! And I thought I was the only one who'd been drinking.

DANE: Thank you, Emile. That was…an interesting synopsis. OK, did any particular chapter or character stand out or strike a chord with anyone? [*a pause*] Sam, what did you think?

SAM: Uh, well… [*pauses in thought*] I have to say, I wasn't really sure what Jon was going on about when he was driving to church. That part escaped me. It seemed he was being a bit hard on himself, wouldn't you say? All that angst over a misplaced book? I mean, I lose track of one thing or another every week, but it doesn't seem to have the same effect on me. Just last week in my office, I couldn't find my pliers when I needed them, but I don't recall having an emotional reaction to the situation.

MARTIN: I'm almost afraid to ask, but why would a vet need pliers?

SAM: Ah, I was treating a young Lab-Cocker Spaniel mix. One of my favorite patients. Very mild disposition. She could stand to lose a pound or two, though. I tell the owner they could both use a few more evening walks. [*chuckles*] She's a bit on the plump side, herself, you see.

MARTIN: Yes, I see. And the pliers?

SAM: Well, it seems she had tried to chew through a tree root while digging a hole and–

MARTIN: [*smirks*] The owner?

SAM: [*unfazed*] No, the dog. And a stick got wedged in the back of her mouth.

MARTIN: And you were going to yank it out with pliers?

SAM: Better the dog bite a pair of pliers than my hand, I always say.

MARTIN: That may be the smartest thing I've heard you say, yet.

SAM: [*sincerely*] Thank you, Martin.

MARTIN: [*enjoying himself*] You're very welcome.

DANE: [*with slight annoyance*] OK, guys, let's get back to our book. Rett, give us your take on the story so far.

RETT: I'll be happy to, Dane. I think what the author is trying to convey in these first few chapters is a man, Jon, struggling to live up to his own expectations of who he is. He likes to see himself in a certain way and wants others to share that perception. But he becomes convicted that it's all an act and remembers his father's admonition to avoid being a phony. And so, he begins to make an effort to find integrity in his life.

MARTIN: Blah, blah, blah. Geez.

RETT: Excuse me?

MARTIN: Blah, blah, blah. Is that what you think it's about?

RETT: [*smiles knowingly*] Martin, as a former pastor, I would say my opinion is more than qualified on the subject. But if you'd like to enlighten us, feel free.

MARTIN: Well, my dear ex-Pastor, you read it, but you clearly don't get it.

RETT: And just what am I missing?

MARTIN: Jon is lost. He hasn't got a clue who he is or why he exists. He looks back on his life and says, "What's the point? I'm alone, and I don't have anyone to love, and no one loves me. If all this God stuff means anything at all, I'm not getting it." And it looks like he's surrounded by a bunch of pretenders who don't get it, either. Except his old pal from college, he gets it. And to our obtuse veterinarian's point, I didn't get the big hubbub around his missing Bible, either. But it sure meant something to Jon. I don't understand it, but I respect how he felt about it. It's a lonely thing being misunderstood. The only thing worse is when you don't understand yourself. And that's where our man Jon was. That's the story I read.

DANE: Wow, thank you, Martin. [*turns with a slight smile to* RETT] Rett, what are your thoughts on that?

RETT: [*shifts slightly in his chair*] Well, of course, if you want to take a purely emotional point of view, I suppose what Martin said would be fitting. But–

MARTIN: How can you not read this from an emotional point of view? Life is all about emotions! How can you experience the world around you if you can't feel it? It's how we know we're alive. Emotion is what separates us from the animals, my dear ex-Pastor. I'm sure even Dr. Dolittle, here, can tell you that.

[*A pause. Everyone looks at* SAM.]

DANE: I think he means you, Sam.

SAM: Huh? Oh, well, I can't speak for cats or rodents, but dogs can be quite expressive. Mostly in their eyes, I find. But, unlike humans, if they show their teeth, it doesn't always mean they're happy. Quite the opposite. It could be anger or stress or thirst or–

MARTIN: You all see my point, don't you? If you can read a story like this and not feel something, maybe something's wrong with you.

RETT: I wasn't trying to imply I didn't feel anything when I read it, Martin.

MARTIN: Ah, it's just expressing emotion that you have a problem with, eh, Pastor?

EMILE: [*to* MARTIN] At least he doesn't need to drink to express himself, dude. For you, alcohol is like some emotional...cat enema.

MARTIN: [*confused*] I'm sorry, a what?

[RETT *holds back a laugh.*]

DANE: Guys, let's take a step back, here. Honestly. It's OK for us to disagree, all right? But let's do it in a respectful way. We're here to encourage each other, not argue.

EMILE: [*gestures toward* MARTIN] Dude, he started it.

DANE: Emile, seriously? Don't make me feel like I'm in my English class at school. We're all adults, here.

EMILE: Fine. Sorry.

DANE: OK. Now, next question for you. [*reads from his notebook*] What do you think about Jon's struggle over the question of why God saved him?

[*A long pause.* RETT *glances around, waiting for someone else to speak.*]

RETT: [*to* DANE] Can I comment on this one?

DANE: [*mildly deflated*] Sure, go ahead, Rett.

RETT: To me, as a former pastor, I found it interesting that a layperson would be having this struggle.

SAM: [*raises his hand*] Uh, I'm sorry. But I'm afraid I haven't heard the term "layperson" before. What exactly is that?

MARTIN: It's how pastors refer to amateur Christians. Like our English lit teacher, here. [*nods toward* DANE]

SAM: Ah, thank you.

RETT: It's not a derogatory term, Martin. I simply meant that I've never seen a church member, casually going about the routine of going to church and Sunday school, suddenly have such a crisis in their faith without some major event occurring in their life, like a death in the family or loss of a job. For it to be the result of simply misplacing their Bible – and feeling such conviction over it – was a bit surprising.

DANE: Are you saying this kind of thing doesn't happen, Rett? That it was unrealistic?

RETT: No, actually, I'm saying it should happen more. Christians should be asking questions like "Why am I here?" because the Bible has answers.

[MARTIN *snickers.*]

DANE: Martin, you have a question about that?

MARTIN: Oh, no, of course not. Who has questions about the Bible?

SAM: Uh….

MARTIN: [*to* SAM] It was a rhetorical question, dear boy. Don't hurt yourself.

EMILE: Well, I've got questions.

DANE: OK, Emile. Go ahead.

EMILE: All right, well, I'm pretty new to all this church stuff. I mean, my mom is Catholic. I mean, like, *crazy* Catholic. But it's always just been about rules to me. And I always seem to be on the wrong side of them, you know? But then something happened to me a few months ago that…kind of…changed everything.

DANE: What happened?

[*A slight pause*]

EMILE: It's kinda hard to talk about, because…people get all freaked-out about it, you know? They sorta…change how they see me.

MARTIN: Let me guess. You robbed a KFC of all their fried chicken. [*laughs*]

EMILE: Dude, I'm gonna let that one go, because I used to work at a KFC before this thing happened, and I like their chicken, OK?

DANE: So, Emile, what exactly happened?

EMILE: Ok, well, my father left us when I was just a baby, see? So, it was just me and my mom growing up. I never met him. But then about eight months ago, I get this certified letter in the mail from some attorney in Oregon. It says my father had died.

DANE: I'm sorry, Emile. I know that had to be hard, even though you didn't know him.

MARTIN: At what point are we supposed to be freaking out? Maybe I missed it.

[DANE *casts an expectant glare at* RETT.]

RETT: [*takes the cue from* DANE] Martin, show a little compassion, will you? [*glances back at* DANE *for approval*]

EMILE: No, that's OK, dude. Because that's not the important part. You see, my dad had moved out West and got into Real Estate and all these investments and stuff. And when he died, he left all his money to me. All of it. That's what the letter was about.

RETT: What did he leave you, Emile?

EMILE: Well, this is the part where people tend to freak out and get all weird and stuff.

DANE: Why? How much was it?

[*A slight pause*]

EMILE: Sixty-three...million.

MARTIN: Dollars?

EMILE: No, dude, Oreos. Of course, dollars.

MARTIN: [*laughs*] You mean to tell me that you [*points at* EMILE] are worth sixty-three million dollars?

EMILE: Well, a little over sixty-four, now. I sold-off one of his properties.

[MARTIN *roars with laughter.*]

EMILE: You see? [*points at* MARTIN] This is what I'm talking about.

DANE: Don't worry about Martin. You said you had some questions about the Bible.

[MARTIN *settles down but continues to giggle to himself, shaking his head.*]

EMILE: Well, my mom believes the money was a miracle. A sign from God, you know? Like some sort of penance for my father leaving us when I was little.

MARTIN: Wait, you're serious? You're actually an unemployed chicken fry-cook multi-millionaire?

EMILE: Dude, believe it if you want. It doesn't matter to me.

MARTIN: It seems I've underestimated you, my rotund friend. I'm impressed.

EMILE: Why? It's not like I earned the money, man. I just got it because my dad died. He did all the work.

DANE: So, Emile, are you wondering if God had something to do with you getting the money?

EMILE: Well, not really. That's my mom's deal. My question is, all my life I've been living day-to-day, week-to-week, trying to get by, worrying about the future. Are we going to have enough money to buy food or pay rent or get gas for the van? Things like that. But now, all of a sudden, I don't have to worry about any of that stuff. I don't even have to work, if I don't want to. And it just made me wonder, what else is there, you know? What's life about if you take away all the stuff that keeps us busy worrying about everything?

RETT: You mean, you asked the same question Jon did in the book: Why am I here?

EMILE: Yeah, sort of. I guess. [*to* DANE] And I like the book so far, man. I didn't think I would, but…it's kinda cool. Long, but….

DANE: I'm glad to hear that, Emile.

EMILE: Yeah, like, it's the first real book I've ever read. Other than graphic novels and that stuff they made me read in school, but those don't count.

DANE: So, then, back to your question: Why am I here? What answer did Jon get to that question in the book?

[EMILE *looks down at his book and flips through its pages.*]

[SAM *raises his hand.*]

DANE: Yes, Sam.

MARTIN: [*puts his hand on* SAM's *knee*] Now, before you answer, you realize the question had nothing to do with animals.

SAM: Uh....

DANE: It's OK, Sam. Go ahead.

SAM: Right. Well, I believe he – Jon, that is – now thinks his reason for being a Christian is to somehow help God make other people Christians, as well. [*looks to* DANE *for confirmation*]

DANE: Exactly.

SAM: [*breathes a sigh of relief*] I must say – like Emile, here – I'm a bit new to all this. So, if I'm off the mark, please just say so.

RETT: You didn't grow-up in a church, Sam?

SAM: No, we lived in a small cottage house, actually.

[MARTIN *sighs audibly.*]

SAM: In the countryside of West Sussex. Just a stone's throw from East Grinstead, south of London.

RETT: [*smiles*] What I meant was: Did you grow-up *going* to church?

SAM: Oh, no. Not at all. There was only one church in East Grinstead. And no one wanted to go there because it had been struck by lightning, once. My mother said God mustn't be very happy with whatever they were doing in there. So, we thought it best to stay away.

DANE: So, how did you come to America?

SAM: Well, I considered making the crossing by ship, but—

MARTIN: Oh, for God's sake, man! No one can be that dim. He meant *why* are you in America, not what mode of transportation brought you here.

SAM: Ah. [*shakes his head at himself*] You see? I'm afraid I'm just not very good at reading between the lines. It leaves me missing the point entirely, sometimes.

MARTIN: [*with sarcasm*] No, really?

SAM: Oh, yes. I get this funny feeling when it's happening, but I usually plow ahead in the wrong direction, just the same.

MARTIN: [*pats* SAM *on the knee*] I think we've discovered your problem with women.

SAM: Really? How so?

MARTIN: [*puts his arm around* SAM's *shoulder*] I'll tell you a secret: The fairer sex lives between the lines.

SAM: They do?

MARTIN: Yes, they do. Just remember: It's not what women say, it's what they want to hear that matters. [*removes his arm from* SAM's *shoulder*] Understand?

SAM: Ah, yes. [*begins nodding in affirmation*] Of course. I see, now. [*pauses in thought*] Actually, I'm not quite clear on all that. Could you go over it one more time?

MARTIN: It's what I was trying to explain to you before. First, you get a bottle of gin and—

DANE: Martin, seriously?

MARTIN: Oh, right. Sorry. Won't happen again.

DANE: [*glances down at his notepad*] I think we've gotten a bit off-track from our discussion. Um….

[*A pause while* DANE *reviews his notes*]

RETT: Dane, if I may?

DANE: [*mildly deflated*] Um, sure.

RETT: [*leans forward in his chair*] Gentlemen, in my years as Pastor of Dead Oak Baptist church in Brouillette, Louisiana, I led many Bible studies and men's groups, such as this. As we get to know each other through our discussion, it's important that we keep our focus on the source material at hand to make the best use of our time. In this case, the book we have in front of us. Now, I believe our last question was around the purpose of Christian faith. Who would like to comment on that?

[*A long, awkward pause*]

DANE: OK, that was helpful. Thank you, Rett.

[RETT *shrinks back in his chair.*]

DANE: Guys, we'll come back to that question later. Let's go in a different direction before we wrap things up for the evening. [*reads from his notes*] Jon faced some temptation in chapter twelve at the football game. How have you dealt with temptation, recently?

MARTIN: Very successfully, thank you. I give in to it every time.

DANE: I guess that shouldn't surprise anyone.

MARTIN: I think of it more as making use of opportunities as they present themselves than giving into temptation.

DANE: OK, so, where does the question of right and wrong come into play?

MARTIN: That's easy. I'm right, and anyone who disagrees with me is wrong. [*smiles in amusement*]

RETT: Martin, I think what Dane is asking is, do you believe in sin?

MARTIN: Ah, sin. I forgot, we are in a church, aren't we? [*leans back in his chair, studies* RETT *and* DANE] You must think I'm quite the unwashed Philistine, don't you? Coming in here, a poor, depraved drunkard stumbling through life. But depravity is such a relative term, isn't it? I mean, it's all in the eyes of the beholding society to determine what behavior is off limits to us mere mortals. You're both upright members of our society, so I respect your obligation to look down your nose at me. But I believe I've chosen a more personally enlightened path: I do whatever makes me happy.

DANE: And does alcohol make you happy, Martin?

MARTIN: Alcohol doesn't do anything but free me to feel however I want to feel. If I want to feel happy, I'm happy. If I want to dig a big hole of misery and bury myself in it, I can do that, too. It's my choice. I drink because it makes it easier to choose how I feel. But look, I don't want to get in trouble with our resident ex-pastor for straying off topic, again, so let's get back to your question about chapter…what was it?

DANE: Chapter twelve. "The Game."

MARTIN: Ah, yes, "The Game." [*laughs with an intentionally maniacal tone*] In chapter twelve, ol' Jonny-boy blames all his ills on alcohol and swears it off in the name of all that's good and decent.

DANE: That's right. And I'm curious to know what you thought about that, Martin.

MARTIN: I thought you might be. But you may find it surprising to learn, good teacher, that I agreed with his decision to hop on the wagon. In fact, I was actually rooting for him to do just that.

DANE: [*surprised*] Why is that? I mean, if you agreed with his decision not to drink anymore out of respect for what's good and decent, why don't you make the same decision for yourself?

MARTIN: Because he had good and decent things to hold onto! A wife who loved him. A little baby who needed him. A respectable profession. I have none of that. I have books to sort and put away and a wife who does the same with me. What do I have to hold onto?

[*A pause*]

EMILE: Dude, how about us?

MARTIN: [*taken aback*] What?

EMILE: How about us? It seems to me you've got four guys, here, who are willing to put up with you for an hour a week, when we really don't even have to. That has to mean something to you.

MARTIN: You're saying you don't mind me being here? You [*points at* EMILE], you don't mind?

EMILE: [*shrugs his shoulders*] Sure, I guess not. If they don't mind, I don't.

[*A pause*]

[MARTIN *appears confused.*]

DANE: Martin, let me ask you something. Why did you come back here this week? You even read the chapters in the book, so I know it wasn't spontaneous.

MARTIN: [*folds his arms in front of him*] I like to read. I am a librarian. Well, a librarian's assistant, at least.

DANE: You like to read? Nothing more than that? You could have gone anywhere if you were trying to avoid an AA meeting. What brought you back here?

[*A slight pause*]

MARTIN: Well, this may come as a shock, but...I don't have any real [*makes air quotes with his fingers*] friends, per se. The only people who really make time for me seem to work for tips. Bartenders and waitresses. They're paid to put up with me. But I make it worth their while, so

51

they listen. But you guys seemed different. You're like normal people. To some degree, at least. [*elbows* SAM] Minus the alcohol.

EMILE: Dude, maybe you don't have any friends because you're a little high maintenance.

[MARTIN *nods in conciliatory agreement.*]

EMILE: Plus, it's like you don't care about anybody, man.

MARTIN: Now, that I object to. I am a very caring person. Ask.... [*pauses in thought*] Well, take my word for it.

EMILE: All right, then why haven't you called any of us by our names since you've been in here? I bet you don't even remember our names, do you?

MARTIN: Of course I do. [*shifts in his chair*] I simply prefer terms of endearment, that's all.

EMILE: OK, [*points at* DANE] what's his name?

MARTIN: He's our group leader and a fine English lit teacher. I refer to him as such out of respect for his leadership.

EMILE: He's Dane. He's Sam. He's Rett. Or Dr. Over-something-or-other. And I'm–

MARTIN: Emile. You're Emile. And that's Dr. Ovaretton T. McCasguill. Of course, I know all your names. There's just four of you.

[*A pause*]

DANE: Then why the act, Martin?

MARTIN: [*sighs*] If you must know, I wasn't too far behind Emile, here, when he came in a little while ago. I was in the hall and heard what he said about me. [*to* EMILE] I heard you say you didn't want me – the drunk guy – in here, because I had issues.

EMILE: Well, you do, dude.

MARTIN: I know I do. I was just hoping maybe you guys...like I said, you seemed different.

DANE: Well…. [*appears uncertain, looks to* RETT]

RETT: Martin, the reason we're here, the reason Dane formed this group, is to point men to faith in Jesus Christ. That's what makes this different than hanging out in a bar talking with strangers. We're not paid to be here. We want to be here to help make life what it's supposed to be.

DANE: [*smiles warmly*] Well said, Rett. And in English, no less.

MARTIN: And what's life supposed to be?

RETT: [*smiles*] Joyful.

MARTIN: [*lets out a laugh*] Joyful? [*shakes his head*] Well, we've got a ways to go then, haven't we?

RETT: Like I said before, life's a journey. Why don't you come along with us, Martin?

SAM: Ah, a metaphor. I got it this time.

[MARTIN *punches* SAM *lightly in the thigh.*]

SAM: [*smiles at the group*] Maybe there's hope for me in the field of romance, after all.

MARTIN: Let's take it one step at a time.

SAM: Right. First, a bottle of gin. I've made a note of that.

[DANE *nods at* MARTIN.]

MARTIN: [*takes the cue from* DANE] No, actually, I was just kidding about the gin, Sam. Scratch that, OK?

SAM: Scratch it. Right. Um….

MARTIN: Just forget about the gin.

SAM: Ah, I see. Yes. It's forgotten. No gin, then.

MARTIN: No gin.

DANE: [*checks the time on his watch*] So, guys, I know we touched on some big issues tonight, but we're out of time for this week.

EMILE: So, like, my little "meaning of life question" will have to wait?

DANE: It's not a small question, Emile, but I promise we'll work towards an answer for you as we go along. So, hang in there, OK?

EMILE: OK, dude.

DANE: All right. So, for next week, I want you to read chapters fourteen through twenty-three. [*looks around the room with expectation*] No groans this time? I guess that's progress. Rett, will you do the honors and close us in prayer?

RETT: Yes, sir.

DANE: Merci. [*smiles and winks at* RETT *as the curtain closes*]

Curtain

ACT ONE

Scene Three

SAM *enters the dark, empty classroom, flips the light switch on the wall and sees the scattering of chairs. As he whistles a playful tune, he reforms the group's semi-circle of chairs with one facing the other four, then quickly folds the remainder and leans them against the wall. He sits down, looks at his watch and waits. After a moment,* MARTIN *enters.*

MARTIN: Where is everyone?

SAM: Ah, Martin. [*stands and offers his hand*] It's just you and me, it seems. At least for the moment. I believe we're both early.

MARTIN: [*shakes* SAM's *hand, then takes a seat*] Maybe they've changed rooms and didn't tell us. That's what I would do if I were them.

SAM: Is that so? You mean, you think they'd want to continue the group without us?

MARTIN: Sure, look at us. We're not exactly top of the class material, are we?

SAM: [*thoughtfully*] No, I suppose not. But I am giving it a go, though. I read the chapters for tonight.

MARTIN: So did I. What did you think?

SAM: [*looks to the door, then back at* MARTIN] Are we allowed to discuss it on our own, or should we wait for the others?

MARTIN: [*pretends to be serious*] I'm sure it's only a minor offense if we get caught. Probably just a warning for the first time.

SAM: Ah…still, perhaps we should wait. No sense in risking it.

MARTIN: [*amused*] No, I guess not. [*studies* SAM *for a moment*] So, you're really a vet, huh?

SAM: Yes. Going on ten years, now.

MARTIN: Went to school, got a degree and everything?

SAM: Oh, yes. Couldn't practice legally without doing that, I'm afraid.

MARTIN: Got decent grades in school, did you?

SAM: Well, not to sound boastful, but I did earn mostly A's.

MARTIN: Really?

SAM: Really. As long as I stuck to the sciences, of course. Biology, chemistry and the like. Those were always my favorites.

MARTIN: So, no psychology or philosophy classes for you, huh?

SAM: Heavens, no. I found out early on the social sciences just weren't for me. Too abstract, I suppose. Not my strength.

MARTIN: [*rubs his chin as he looks at* SAM] No.

SAM: I prefer things straight on. Easier that way. [*perks up*] I guess that's why I enjoy treating animals. It's just very matter of fact, you know?

MARTIN: And they can hardly argue with your diagnosis.

SAM: [*enthused*] Exactly! Though, I must say, their owners can be a very different story, sometimes. But, on the whole, most are very pleasant. One actually invited me to come to this church.

MARTIN: Really? And was this particular pet owner a woman, by chance?

SAM: Yes, how did you know?

MARTIN: And I'm guessing she owns a cat, right?

SAM: [*nods in affirmation*] That's remarkable.

MARTIN: [*shrugs*] It's a gift.

SAM: I saw her again this morning, actually. Third time in three weeks, I believe.

MARTIN: She was in your office three weeks in a row?

SAM: Yes.

MARTIN: And did she seem upset or bothered that she had to see you again, this morning?

SAM: [*appears a bit confused*] We are talking about the cat, aren't we?

MARTIN: [*chuckles*] No, the owner.

MARTIN: Oh, well, she's always very pleasant anytime she comes in. And she is one of my more frequent clients, come to think of it.

MARTIN: And she invited you to come to her church.

SAM: Yes.

MARTIN: Sam, are you certain her cat is the reason she's been in your office three weeks in a row?

SAM: Oh, yes, definitely. She does have a dog, but I haven't seen him since the last time he ate a nylon stocking.

MARTIN: I think you're missing a few clues, here Sam, old boy. [DANE *enters followed by* RETT, *who holds a Starbucks coffee cup in his hand.*]

DANE: [*to* RETT] That's not a macchiato.

RETT: It is, too! It's a caramel macchiato. I can show you the receipt. [*pulls a receipt from his pocket*] Here, it says, "Triple Venti Half Sweet Non-Fat Caramel Macchiato."

DANE: [*laughs*] Rett, I don't care what Starbucks calls it; they're the Taco Bell of coffee. What you're holding in your hand is a cup of iced milk with a tiny shot of cheap espresso in it. A real macchiato is an espresso shot with just a spot of milk. It's the exact opposite from what you're drinking.

RETT: Well, it happens to be quite good, regardless. Je ne care pas. [*sits down next to* MARTIN] Hey, Martin.

MARTIN: [*nods*] Pastor.

DANE: [*to* RETT] I can't decide what I hate worse: your taste in coffee or your French. [*to* SAM *and* MARTIN] Hey, guys. Sorry I'm late. [*sits down in the chair facing the others*] Parent-teacher conference went a little long and then traffic across town.

MARTIN: No worries. Sam and I were just decoding some hidden signals from a certain lady admirer of his.

DANE: Oh, really? Who, Sam?

SAM: [*confused*] Well, I'm not quite sure. Who, Martin?

MARTIN: Oh, come on, Sam. Do I have to spell it out for you?

SAM: That would be helpful, yes.

MARTIN: Your cat owner has a crush on you. Can't you see that?

SAM: Uh....

DANE: Is this the constipated cat with the infected paw?

MARTIN: You know this woman's cat?

DANE: No, he's told us about it the last two weeks. I guess you missed that.

MARTIN: How does a cat get constipated?

SAM: Well–

MARTIN: She probably fed it a block of cheese just to have an excuse to come see you.

SAM: I suppose cheese could slow things down a bit, but in this case—

DANE: I hate to change the subject, guys – actually, I'm happy to change the subject – but since we're starting late, maybe we should go ahead and get things going. [*opens his notebook on his lap*]

RETT: What's the rush? Where's Emile?

MARTIN: [*quietly to* SAM] We'll talk later. [*winks*]

[SAM *nods in affirmation and returns a deliberate wink.*]

RETT: He's not joining us this week?

DANE: I haven't heard from him. So I don't know.

MARTIN: We haven't seen him. Not that we could miss him.

RETT: Martin, you seem a little more...composed this week.

MARTIN: Ah, well, I didn't make any stops for adult refreshments on the way here this time, if that's what you mean.

DANE: So, we get the real Martin, this week, huh?

MARTIN: No, you've had the real Martin the last two weeks. This week, I'm not sure what you'll get. But I'm here.

[EMILE *enters, hurriedly and out of breath.*]

EMILE: Hey. Sorry I'm late. [*plops down heavily on the end chair next to* RETT]

DANE: Catch your breath, Emile. We were just getting started. You OK?

EMILE: [*still panting*] Yeah...I'm fine.

MARTIN: [*looks at* EMILE] Running after the ice cream truck, again, were you?

EMILE: Dude, already? I just sat down, and you're ragging on me.

SAM: We have ice cream?

DANE: Martin, I was hoping you'd be a little less...sarcastic, considering.

EMILE: Considering what?

RETT: Martin didn't imbibe before joining us, tonight.

EMILE: You're not drunk this week, man?

59

MARTIN: No, I'm afraid not. But I can always slip out for a few cocktails and come back, if you'd prefer.

EMILE: No, this is good. I was wondering what you were like sober.

MARTIN: I get that a lot.

DANE: OK, guys, we're all here, so let's get started. First, a little icebreaker.

[MARTIN *groans*.]

DANE: In our reading for this week, we got to meet some people from our main character's past. So, here's a question for each of you: [*reads from his notebook*] Name one person from your past that you wish you could spend ten minutes with today, and what would you say to them? Emile, why don't we start with you?

EMILE: Like, who do you mean? Does it have to be a real person? Or can it be like a character from a movie or a graphic novel or something?

DANE: A real person would be good.

EMILE: Does he have to be alive? Or can he be, like, you know…not living, anymore?

MARTIN: For goodness sake, man, it's just a conversation starter. You're not negotiating a contract.

DANE: It can be anyone you want, Emile.

EMILE: OK, well…I guess I would have to say my dad, then.

DANE: OK. And what would you say to your dad?

EMILE: Well, I never got to talk to him, except for when I was a baby. And I couldn't talk then, anyway, except for like goo-goo-gah-gah kind of stuff. Not that I remember that.

DANE: So, what would you say to him, today?

EMILE: I think I'd tell him, "Don't sweat it, man."

RETT: Why would you say that, Emile?

DANE: Yeah, what do you mean?

EMILE: Well, he left me all his money, right? So, I figure he did that because he felt guilty about ditching me and my mom. And never even sending me so much as a birthday card for twenty-four years. So, like, I would just tell him, "Don't worry about it. I turned out OK." I guess I just don't like the idea of him feeling bad about things.

RETT: That's very forgiving of you.

EMILE: Yeah, well. Regret sucks, dude. So, I'd rather not make anybody feel that way.

DANE: Thanks for sharing that, Emile. Sam, how about you? Who would you like to spend ten minutes with?

SAM: Sarah Pondsickle.

MARTIN: [chuckles] Sarah *Pondsickle? Pondsickle?*

DANE: Is she a girl you knew growing up? Or in college, Sam?

SAM: Oh, no. She's a client at my veterinary practice.

MARTIN: Ah-ha! Now we're getting somewhere. Is this the same cat woman we just talked about?

SAM: No. Well, she does have a cat. But hers is of the more feral variety. He just appeared one day on her stoop and hasn't left since. Doesn't even have a real name, just Kitty. But she rarely brings him in to see me. Just whenever she can catch him, I suppose.

DANE: When was the last time you saw Sarah, Sam?

SAM: Yesterday.

EMILE: [to DANE] Dude, I thought we were supposed to say somebody from our past.

DANE: [nods] Well, technically, yesterday is in the past, Emile.

MARTIN: So, come on, Sam. Tell us about Sarah. I'm beginning to wonder if you have a whole clientele of lonely female pet owners making up lame pet problems just to see their favorite British veterinarian. And I'm willing to bet her cat wasn't the reason she came to see you, either.

SAM: Well, I don't know how you know these things, Martin, but you are right about that.

MARTIN: I knew it!

SAM: Yesterday, she brought in her dog, Melvin.

[MARTIN *sighs.*]

SAM: He hasn't been eating well. Has a sore tooth, I'm afraid. It's no fun biting down on a kibble with a bad premolar, I assure you.

MARTIN: [*defeated*] I wouldn't know.

DANE: Martin, let me see if I can help. Sam, I'm guessing you like this woman?

SAM: Oh, yes. Very much. She pays promptly, never cancels her appointments.

DANE: And if you could spend ten minutes alone with her – without her pets – what would you like to say to her?

SAM: Well, funny you should ask. I've actually given this a lot of thought since she was in yesterday. [*pauses*]

DANE: And?

SAM: I think I'd tell her – in the firmest way, mind you – that she needs to be brushing Melvin's teeth.

MARTIN: [*drops his head*] Good lord, man.

SAM: I know it's not pleasant for either one of them, but gum disease is a serious canine concern.

DANE: [*chuckles*] OK, well, good luck with that, Sam.

SAM: Yes, thank you.

DANE: [*smiles toward* MARTIN] Martin, I tried. And you're next. Who would you like to spend ten minutes with, and what would you say?

MARTIN: Hmm. Let me start by saying, I noticed in the book that our man Jon seems to have the same problem Sam, here, has.

DANE: What's that?

SAM: Yes, to what problem are you referring?

MARTIN: He doesn't seem to know what to do when opportunity presents itself.

DANE: You're talking about Jon's friendship with Amy?

MARTIN: That's one example. I don't know why he didn't take her up on her invitation at the beach. But actually, I was referring to Jenny.

EMILE: You want to spend your ten minutes with a fictional character? I thought we couldn't do that.

MARTIN: Relax. I don't want to spend time with a character from the book. I had my own "Jenny," of sorts. Her name was Emma. We dated when I was in college; I was crazy about her. But she broke it off with me, and I never knew why.

DANE: So, if you had ten minutes with her, is that what you would ask? Why she broke-up with you?

MARTIN: More or less. I can't really blame her, though. Based on what you see sitting here today, you'd have to say she made the right call, don't you? I'd just like to know what tipped her off.

DANE: What do you mean?

MARTIN: I mean, what did she see in me back then that told her I was a bad risk? Maybe, if I had known, I could have changed something. I could have made her happy.

EMILE: You see? This is what I was talking about. Regret sucks, man. Don't do it to yourself.

MARTIN: I disagree. Regret is the fuel that drives our desire to get it right the next time. You take away all regret and we end up stumbling through life frying chickens at a KFC.

EMILE: Hey, man, I'm doing all right.

MARTIN: Yes, thanks to your late, regret-filled, estranged father. You just made my point for me.

DANE: Guys, the question is obviously geared towards dealing with reconciliation or missed opportunities in our past. How we deal with those is up to us. There's no right answer here. Rett, how about you? Who would you pick?

RETT: [*crosses his legs*] Well, this is an easy one for me, Dane. I would like to spend my ten minutes with my favorite professor from seminary, Dr. Philmore.

DANE: And what would you like to say to Dr. Philmore?

RETT: I would just thank him for helping me become the man I am today.

DANE: And just who is that, exactly, Rett?

RETT: I'm sorry?

DANE: How would you describe the man you are today?

RETT: Well, I'm the former Pastor of Dead Oak Baptist Church in–

DANE: Brouillette, Louisiana. Right. We've got that part. But that's who you were. Tell us about the man you are today.

RETT: [*uncrosses his legs and pushes himself straight in his chair*] Well, I'm...uh...I'm...in a state of transition, now, Dane. You know that. I'm just....

[*A pause*]

DANE: I'm sorry if that caught you off-guard, Rett. I was just interested in how you see yourself now that you're out of the ministry.

RETT: [*meekly*] No, it's certainly a fair question. A man faithfully serves as pastor of a small but growing church for a number of years and then moves on.... It's only natural for people to have questions about that.

EMILE: Yeah, dude, why'd you leave? I thought being a pastor was like...permanent or something. Like the Supreme Court.

RETT: Well, Emile, in some cases, a pastor does serve a particular congregation until he retires. But sometimes—

EMILE: Can they, like, fire you if they want?

RETT: [*chuckles uncomfortably*] Well, that all depends. Some churches have leadership committees and written bylaws with certain conditions. And if a pastor were to violate those conditions, say for breach of trust or some act that dishonored the integrity of the pastoral position, then they could, if the committee chose to, request that their pastor step down for the good of the church as a whole. Or...they could put it to a vote and let the congregation decide. [*eyes look down*]

[*Awkward pause as everyone looks at* RETT]

DANE: I tell you what, that question took a little more time than I thought it would, so let's go ahead and talk about the chapters for this week. [*quickly turns a page in his notebook*] First, we see Jon getting dumped by his college girlfriend, Jenny, as Martin already alluded to. What was her reason for ending their relationship?

EMILE: He wasn't Christian enough.

DANE: That was tough for Jon to hear, wasn't it?

MARTIN: At least he got a reason.

DANE: That's true. But is there a sliding scale of how Christian someone can be? Or is it more of a yes or no

65

proposition? Either you are one, or you aren't. [*a pause*] Sam, what do you think?

SAM: I'm not sure I'm best qualified to answer.

DANE: It's OK. Just give it your best shot.

SAM: All right. I will say that it appears from Jon's discussion with his daughter, Holly – and his own struggles in previous chapters – that there seems to be some difference between perceiving oneself as a Christian and actually being one. Although, I'm not quite clear on the mechanics of either position.

EMILE: I don't know about all that, but the part I was curious about was the whole "God speaking to Jon in the bathtub" thing. What's up with that?

DANE: Well, Emile, I believe that goes back to your question from last week, doesn't it?

EMILE: I asked if God speaks to us in bathtubs?

DANE: No, you were wondering what life was about if you took away all the stuff you had to worry about.

EMILE: Oh, yeah, that.

DANE: It's basically the same question Jon wrestled with, just in reverse. He figured out his purpose but then had to get past all the worries that kept him from living it out. That's what he was praying about in the bathtub.

EMILE: Yeah, but I don't hear God speaking to me and telling me to go off and do stuff.

DANE: [*to the group*] What did you guys think about that? When Jon felt God speaking to him through Scripture, did you buy that? [*a pause*] Rett, you're awfully quiet. What do you think?

RETT: [*clears his throat*] Well, Sam and Emile have raised some interesting questions.

[*A slight pause as* RETT *adjusts himself in his chair*]

RETT: First, in my experience, Sam, often one of the biggest challenges in bringing someone to faith is getting them to see past a long-held self-perception that tells them they already are a Christian when they really aren't, by God's definition. It's not the Gospel they reject; it's the notion that they aren't already saved by it that gives them trouble. It's a tough sell and one that leaves many people in our churches without a saving relationship with Christ. It's easier for a flat-out non-believer to see his lost condition and need for God's forgiveness and saving grace than someone who clings with pride to a label pressed upon them by their parents or a church that doesn't clearly preach the Gospel. [*turns to* EMILE] And then to your question about God speaking to us. That's what the Bible is, Emile. It's God speaking to us through his written Word. So, certainly, God speaks to us that way. But to the question of God speaking to Jon in the bathtub, as I remember, a verse of Scripture came to Jon as he lay quietly in the tub. He took that verse as direction and an answer to his prayer. I firmly believe that when you combine reading and study of Scripture with the Holy Spirit at work in the mind and heart of a Believer, God can and does speak to us, just as it happened in the book.

EMILE: Wow, dude. You really are a pastor.

RETT: I was a pastor, Emile. [*glances at* DANE] Now, I'm not sure what I am.

DANE: Is that something you want to talk about, Rett?

RETT: No. How about we just stick to the book. What's next?

DANE: Well, [*looks down at his notes*] I was going to ask about Jon's decision to leave his job to go share the Gospel with people. If someone you worked with came to you and told you they were doing what Jon did, what would you say?

MARTIN: I'd tell them they were either brave, stupid or insane. Either of those three conditions could drive the same behavior.

DANE: But wouldn't you want to know which of those was the real driving factor?

MARTIN: Well, since there is no such thing as a brave librarian, if it were anyone I work with, I'm sure it would be one of the latter two possibilities.

DANE: And you'd be OK with that?

MARTIN: Sure. One less stupid or crazy person to put up with every day is fine by me.

DANE: All right, that's not quite the answer I was hoping for, but…Sam, how about you? What would you say if one of your staff members decided to do what Jon did?

SAM: I suppose I'd say, "Best of luck. Fingers crossed. Ring me when you get back." Or something of the sort.

DANE: Right, but would you have any thoughts or opinions about what they'd be doing?

[*A pause*]

[SAM *looks puzzled.*]

MARTIN: [*to* DANE] I think you've lowered your bucket in a dry well.

EMILE: I can't speak for Sam, and I don't really work with anyone right now in a job or anything, or know anyone who would do what Jon did, but–

MARTIN: Now that you've fully disqualified yourself from having a valid opinion, please continue.

EMILE: Dude, you know, you're almost the same sober as you are drunk.

MARTIN: [*pleased with himself*] I take that as a compliment. Thank you.

DANE: You were saying, Emile?

EMILE: Oh, yeah, I was just going to say that if someone told me they were doing what Jon decided to do in the book, I'd be like, why? I mean, there's plenty of churches out there. And it's not like people haven't heard of God before, you know? I guess I don't see where quitting your job just to go tell a few people to go to church is all that necessary. If they want to go to church or not, it's up to them, isn't it?

DANE: I think most people today would agree with you, Emile. But isn't that some of what Jon wrestled with? Just going to church? What did he come to believe he was missing from that?

SAM: I believe he said he was missing the purpose for going to church, which he then surmised to be telling people about Jesus.

MARTIN: Wow. Blood from a turnip.

DANE: That's right, Sam. Jon's motivation, or calling, wasn't to just get people to go to church. There are lots of reasons people go to church. Can you guys name a few?

RETT: To worship God, learn about his character, hear the truth in his Word, find meaning in life, experience his grace and love, just to name a few.

MARTIN: Sounds like you're reading from a sales brochure.

RETT: All right, Martin, what would you say, then?

MARTIN: Well, let's see if we can make your brochure sound more realistic. How about: If you're single and can't get a date elsewhere, come to church. Or, if you're a businessman looking for new clients, come to church. Or, if you need a place to ditch your kids for a couple hours, come to church. Or – my favorite – if you want to pretend you're better than everyone else, come to church.

DANE: That's a pretty cynical view of people in church, Martin. Is that how you see it?

MARTIN: Jesus himself said, "Narrow is the way, which leadeth unto life, and few there be that find it." I always find it amusing when Jesus talks like Jack Sparrow.

DANE: Martin, you know Scripture?

RETT: You've read the Bible?

MARTIN: You ask that like I've stolen something. It's not your Bible, you know. We do keep copies in the public library.

RETT: I know, but–

MARTIN: But how can someone have read the same Bible as you and still be a heathen like me? Isn't that what you're thinking?

RETT: I'm just surprised, that's all. If someone has made a study of Scripture, enough to quote the King James Bible, I would've expected there to be some evidence of….

MARTIN: I told you before; I like to read. But reading the Bible doesn't make me a churchgoer any more than reading romantic poetry makes me John Keats. I simply enjoy good literature. Does that offend your ex-pastor sensibilities?

RETT: No, it's just... [shakes his head] frustrating.

DANE: How so, Rett?

RETT: Dane, as a pastor, I spent most of my time trying to get people who were already in church to read their Bible – you know, that thick book they carry around with them on Sunday mornings but never open any other time – hoping that if they read what God has to say to them, it would change their lives. And now, in stumbles Martin, literally, his life a self-professed drunken mess – no offense–

MARTIN: None taken.

RETT: –happily quoting Scripture to me. It's enough to make a man....

DANE: Leave the ministry?

RETT: No, that's not what I was going to say.

DANE: Make a man what, then?

RETT: Tu me rends assez fâché à cracher.

DANE: What the heck does that mean?

RETT: It means I'm mad enough to spit.

DANE: Well, then just say that!

RETT: I did.

DANE: In English! [*sighs*] Honestly.

RETT: And the maddening part is that Martin's right.

MARTIN: I'm sorry?

RETT: The reasons I gave for being in church are what I believe to be the right ones. But the truth is closer to what Jon was saying in the book. A lot of people are in church for the wrong reasons. And when you try and push them out of their comfort zone to help them see the Truth, sometimes they push back.

EMILE: But, dude, if everybody who goes to church dropped what they were doing and did what Jon says he's going to do in the book, there wouldn't be anybody left in church.

RETT: Emile, if I were a pastor of a church and no one showed up one Sunday morning because they were all out sharing the Gospel with people, I would be the happiest man in the world. I can't imagine anything greater than that. I would have done my job.

MARTIN: Ah, but "not forsaking the assembling of ourselves together, as the manner of some is." *Arrr.* [*giggles*]

RETT: Martin, that's going to get really annoying.

MARTIN: [*grins devilishly*] I've got more, if you want to hear it.

RETT: That's what I'm afraid of.

DANE: OK, I think this might be a good time for us to stop for tonight.

EMILE: Dude, it was just starting to get interesting.

DANE: You'll just have to come back next week, Emile. Rett, would you like to close us in prayer?

RETT: I think I'll pass tonight, Dane.

DANE: Um, OK. Anyone else? [*glances at* MARTIN *and raises an eyebrow*]

MARTIN: [*taken aback*] Don't look at *me.*

DANE: [*laughs*] I was almost hoping you would just to see what you'd say.

MARTIN: I'm sure it would shock both of us.

DANE: Another time, maybe. But I'll do the honors, tonight.

[*The group bows their heads to pray and the curtain closes.*]

Curtain

ACT TWO

Scene One

SAM *enters the dark, empty classroom and flips the light switch on the wall. Seeing the scattering of chairs, he reforms their semi-circle of chairs with one facing the others, then quickly folds the remainder and leans them against the wall. He sits down, looks at his watch and waits. After a moment,* MARTIN *enters appearing somewhat unsteady.*

MARTIN: Ah, so we meet again: the phlegmatic vet and the dashingly handsome assistant librarian.

SAM: Hello, Martin. [*stands and offers his hand*] We appear to be on the same schedule the last two weeks. Early, I mean.

MARTIN: [*ignores* SAM's *offer of a handshake and takes a seat two chairs away from him*] Well, it's intentional on my part. I was hoping to catch you alone for a moment before our esteemed cohorts in literary discourse arrive.

SAM: [*studies* MARTIN *for a moment*] I apologize if this seems an invasive question, Martin, but...have you been drinking, again?

MARTIN: I accept your apology, and yes, I have treated myself to more than one adult beverage this evening.

SAM: After last week, I was rather hoping you had moved on from all that.

MARTIN: My condition last week was a rare occurrence, a faint blip on the radar screen of sobriety. I seriously doubt you'll have the misfortune of seeing me that way again.

73

SAM: I'm sorry to hear that.

MARTIN: Anyway, I wanted to talk with you about something I'm sure you'll find very interesting.

SAM: Yes, of course. I'm listening.

MARTIN: That's a good boy. You'll never guess who I had the pleasure of meeting last week in the library.

SAM: All right. Who?

MARTIN: No, you see, here's where you're supposed to try and prove me wrong by guessing correctly. So go ahead, guess.

SAM: Well, I–

MARTIN: Your cat woman.

SAM: [*furrows his brow in thought*] Ms. Pondsickle?

MARTIN: [*giggles*] No, the other one.

SAM: Ms. Walker?

MARTIN: Is that what you call her? Ms. Walker? She's far too young and attractive to be called Ms. Walker. That's what you'd call an old maid librarian.

SAM: Well, she is a client. I must keep it professional, you know. I'm not sure it would be appropriate to address her with such familiarity as to call her Hannah. [*eyes drift-up in thought*] Lovely name, though – Hannah. [*quickly regains his focus on* MARTIN] No, decorum dictates otherwise. Unless, of course, she makes a specific request that I call her Hannah. Which, come to think of it, she may have. I'm not sure. How did you...where did you meet her?

MARTIN: I told you; she came into my library.

SAM: Yes, but I'm sure many women come into your library each day. How in the world did you know she was my cat woman? I mean, my client Ms. Walker?

MARTIN: Well, she walked up to the reference desk and placed two books on the counter. And I immediately suspected who she might be.

SAM: I find that rather hard to fathom. How could you possibly know?

MARTIN: It was easy. She was returning *Romancing Mister Bridgerton* and checking out *Edward the Conqueror*.

SAM: I fail to see how her choice of books could lead you to conclude that I'm her veterinarian.

MARTIN: They didn't. She told me that. But they did tell me enough about her to ask the right questions.

SAM: I'm afraid I don't understand.

MARTIN: Sam, if you were a student of literature instead of house pets, you'd know that Julia Quinn is a romance novelist known for stories of unrequited love, something I suspect our beautiful Ms. Walker relates to very well. So, the fact that she'd just read *Romancing Mister Bridgerton* was my first clue. And of course, Roald Dahl's *Edward the Conqueror* is a must read for any true cat lover.

SAM: Fascinating.

MARTIN: You really should read more, Sam.

SAM: Yes, I suppose I should. Please, go on.

MARTIN: So, being a librarian of keen wit and intellect, I put two and two together and asked if she had a cat. Of course, she said yes. Then, I told her my cat was having a bout of constipation and asked if she knew a good vet. She became very excited, saying her cat had just been treated for the same thing and volunteered your name. Voila! Your cat woman!

SAM: What kind of cat do you have, Martin?

MARTIN: [*incredulous*] After what I just told you, that's what you want to know? If I have a cat?

SAM: Well, you did say—

MARTIN: Forget the cat. I lied about having a cat.

SAM: Oh. Uh....

MARTIN: But I still haven't gotten to the best part of the story.

SAM: There's more?

MARTIN: Oh, yes. Much more. Your Ms. Walker is going to meet me this weekend for a drink.

SAM: [*sternly*] Martin, I must protest!

MARTIN: Why?

SAM: [*with shrinking assertiveness*] Well, after all, you...have a wife.

MARTIN: What's that got to do with anything?

SAM: Married men shouldn't meet young, attractive women for drinks. Unless, of course, they happen to be their wives.

MARTIN: Where's the fun in that?

SAM: Martin, you're a married man. Surely that must mean something to you.

MARTIN: I believe you omitted a very important adverb: I'm an *unhappily* married man.

SAM: It makes no difference. It's terribly improper of you.

MARTIN: Ah, but you see, those of us men who are unhappily married have great license to do whatever it is we want, as opposed to those who are just happily married. It's a totally different arrangement. It's very liberating, in fact.

SAM: Yes, but—

[DANE *enters.*]

DANE: Hey, guys.

SAM: [*flustered*] Hello, Dane.

[DANE *takes his seat in the leader's chair.*]

DANE: What's wrong, Sam?

MARTIN: Tell me, Sam, are you upset that I'm married? Or is it that, maybe, you're just a bit jealous of ol' Martin.

SAM: I'm sure I don't know what you mean.

MARTIN: Oh, I'm sure you do.

DANE: What's this all about?

SAM: [*sits straight in his chair*] Martin, you'll forgive me, but: [*points at* MARTIN] Dane – Martin, here, has made a date with a woman other than his wife. And I strongly object.

MARTIN: [*smiles*] Tell him who it is, Sam.

[EMILE *enters.*]

EMILE: Hey. What's up, guys?

SAM: [*ignores* EMILE's *entrance*] She's a client of mine.

[EMILE *sits down between* SAM *and* MARTIN.]

MARTIN: [*to* DANE] It's his cat woman.

DANE: [*to* SAM] The woman who invited you to come to church here?

SAM: I'm afraid so.

MARTIN: [*grins*] Her name's Hannah. And she's quite fetching, isn't she, Sam?

SAM: Yes, I suppose she is. But that has little to do with the real issue, here.

MARTIN: That is the real issue.

EMILE: What's going on? Did I miss something, already?

[RETT *enters.*]

RETT: Gentlemen! Greetings!

DANE: Hey, Rett. Come on in.

[RETT *sits next to* MARTIN.]

DANE: Martin, have you been drinking, again?

RETT: Uh-oh.

MARTIN: Of course, I've been drinking. Birds fly, don't they? Fish swim. And men who can't please their wives drink. I'm simply obeying the laws of nature.

DANE: I take it you've had a bad day.

MARTIN: I'll put it in perspective for you: I expect the next hour to be the highlight of my week.

DANE: Anything you want to talk about?

MARTIN: Always, but I'll wait and drop it on you when you least expect it.

DANE: Thanks for the warning.

EMILE: [*to* MARTIN] Are you sure you're OK to be here, dude? This is a church, you know. You don't want lightning to strike or something.

SAM: [*nods*] It has happened before.

MARTIN: You should all be happy I'm here. "They that are whole have no need of the physician, but they that are sick," says I. [*giggles*]

RETT: There he goes again, quoting Scripture like he's Johnny Depp.

MARTIN: Avast, there, ex-Pastor!

DANE: OK, Martin, tone it down a bit, will you? Sam, do we need to talk through what you were upset about?

SAM: I'd prefer we just move on. Martin knows full well my position on the matter. I trust his conscience will do the rest.

EMILE: [*to* SAM] Uh, dude, [*points at* MARTIN] I'm not sure he has one.

MARTIN: Perhaps, you could buy one for me, Colonel Sanders.

EMILE: If I could, I would, man!

DANE: Guys, guys...let's just hit the reset button and relax. OK? Everybody chill. [*looks at* RETT] Geez.

RETT: [*shrugs*] Must be a full moon or something.

DANE: All right, well, let's try and get on topic. Did everyone read the chapters for this week?

[*All nod in the affirmative, except* MARTIN.]

DANE: Martin, how about you?

MARTIN: Oh, yes. I read them. And I particularly enjoyed the arguments Jon and his late wife had about alcohol. [*with sarcasm*] Isn't that just an amazing coincidence? It's left me wondering if my being here these last few weeks wasn't somehow the underhanded work of my wife. I wouldn't put it past her. Here I'd thought it was my decision to join your little group and read this emotional yarn of endless prayers and divine interventions. But now, I'm beginning to feel a bit manipulated.

DANE: I can assure you, Martin, your wife has nothing to do with you being here. I'm assuming she still thinks you're at an AA meeting right now.

MARTIN: It doesn't matter. I doubt she even realizes I'm not home.

DANE: Well, we're, um…glad you're here. [*gives a nod to* RETT]

MARTIN: You don't mean that.

DANE: Sure, I do. You need involvement.

MARTIN: An English lit teacher who quotes from the *Peanuts' Christmas Special*. A true renaissance man.

  [RETT *laughs.*]

DANE: I'm glad you enjoyed that, Rett. [*to the group*] OK, I'm going to skip the icebreaker I had planned for tonight, since you guys seem warmed-up enough, already. And, since Martin's already opened up our discussion with his thoughts on what we read, does anyone else have any initial comments? What jumped out at you?

EMILE: Dude, Lacey died. That sucked.

MARTIN: Surely, you saw that coming. It was telegraphed from the second chapter on.

EMILE: No, man. I just thought she dumped him and took-off with somebody else. I didn't think she was, you know, dead or anything. Poor guy.

MARTIN: Poor fictional guy. It's not real, Emile.

EMILE: But it could be. Stuff like that really happens. You know, drinking and driving. How did *you* get here, by the way?

MARTIN: Well, the part between the bar and the church is a little sketchy, but I assume I drove here.

DANE: Well, you're not driving home. Trust me on that.

MARTIN: I'll defer that argument to my future self. He may have a different opinion than I do at the moment.

DANE: That's fine. Sam let's start our discussion with you. What thoughts did you have from what you read?

SAM: Ah, well, um...first, I would say that Jon isn't quite the sympathetic character I had originally assumed him to be.

DANE: How so, Sam?

SAM: Well, I may not be reading this correctly, but it seemed to me that he was the source of much of the conflict between him and his wife. I know he's our protagonist, but I found him to be rather indifferent to his wife's feelings and interests.

DANE: Are you talking about before or after his salvation experience, Sam?

SAM: From what I can tell, both before and after. The story does jump around a bit.

MARTIN: [*to* SAM] But why are you taking her side? What about Jon's needs? What about his feelings and his interests?

SAM: You do have a point. But I just found myself feeling sorry for her. Crying alone on the floor like that.

DANE: You've been reading ahead.

SAM: Just a bit. But don't you think Jon seemed a bit harsh with her at times? I can't imagine being so brash with my wife. If I were married, that is, which I'm certainly not. And then for Lacey to expire that way. It was all rather upsetting.

MARTIN: Our author does seem to enjoy making his readers cry. Perhaps your imaginary wife would enjoy reading it after you finish.

EMILE: Yeah, but Sam, I don't think Jon was being that way on purpose. He kinda knew he was being a jerk. After the fact, I mean. I think he felt bad about it.

DANE: OK, let me ask you guys: How much of that conflict do you think resulted from Jon's faith, specifically? Both with Lacey and with his friend Brant?

EMILE: All of it. Before he got all serious about his faith, he had a good friend and a hot wife. And then afterwards he had neither. I mean, it's like he was cursed all of a sudden, man.

SAM: I'm rather curious about that. Is this the sort of thing people who call themselves Christian have to deal with? It seems quite disruptive.

RETT: Dane, may I answer this one?

DANE: It's all yours.

RETT: Sam, first, you have to take into account the fact that the character in question was very young in his faith and was not involved in a church where he could be discipled in the sanctification process. Second, his enthusiasm for sharing his faith was matched only by his spiritual immaturity and lack of tact. It's only natural to expect relational conflict in such situations.

SAM: [*thoughtfully*] Ah...I see. Of course. Yes, thank you.

DANE: Did that answer your question, Sam?

81

SAM: Uh….

MARTIN: That's "Sam" for no.

EMILE: Yeah, but it kind of makes you want to not do the whole born again thing, if that's what it's like.

DANE: Do you think that's what the author was trying to convey, Emile?

EMILE: Well, no. I guess not.

DANE: So, then, why do you think he included storylines that show some of the difficulties that come along with the Christian faith?

MARTIN: Because most Christians have a persecution complex, that's why. They think the whole world is against them, when the world really just wants to be left alone.

DANE: Is that what you want, Martin? To be left alone?

MARTIN: I am alone.

DANE: No, you're sitting among friends in a Christian church, talking about a Christian novel, written by a Christian author, about what it's like to be a real Christian. If you wanted to be left alone from all that, I don't think you'd be here.

EMILE: [*smiles eagerly*] Oh, snap!

MARTIN: [*glares at* EMILE] Snap? Seriously?

RETT: Martin, let me ask you something. When you read the chapter, "The Cowboy Preacher"–

SAM: Oh! Who is – I'm sorry to interrupt – but who is Cameron Parsons? Should I have heard of him, before?

DANE: He's just a fictional character, Sam. There is no real Cam Parsons.

RETT: The author used Cam Parsons to represent some sort of Billy Graham-type evangelist. You've heard of him, haven't you, Sam?

SAM: Oh, yes, absolutely.

MARTIN: What kind of cat would you say he has, Sam?

SAM: [*gives it serious thought*] I don't know. But, if I had to guess, I'd say he's more of a dog man than a cat owner. Though, no one really owns a cat, I always say. Rather, I could see him with a nice Labrador retriever. They're very loyal animals, you know.

MARTIN: [*grins*] Yes. Tell us more, Sam.

SAM: Well, as a breed, they–

DANE: Sam, I think Martin was just trying to avoid Rett's question. He wasn't serious.

SAM: Oh...sorry.

DANE: That's OK. Go ahead, Rett.

RETT: Thank you, Dane. Anyway, Martin, what did you feel as you read that sermon and saw Jon make his decision for Christ? Anything?

MARTIN: Well, unlike Jon, I suffer from no delusions of being a Christian, false or otherwise. So, if you're asking if I felt compelled to throw myself on the bathroom floor, as he did, and confess my sins after reading that chapter, the answer would be no. But it did go a long way in explaining the change in his character. What I found more interesting was his chat with Amy a few chapters later.

DANE: On Facebook?

MARTIN: Yes. What was the idiot thinking? I would've hopped in my car that very night and driven down to see that poor girl. Why wait six months? Even Sam, here, might have figured that one out.

DANE: Jon felt that God was using Amy to test his resolve. And he chose to stay committed to his trip.

MARTIN: Yes, but you can't put romance on the back burner and expect it to be there waiting for you six months later. Women are like cut flowers. You better enjoy them while they're blooming. [*grins*] Like Hannah, right, Sam?

SAM: Now, see here, Martin. Ms. Walker is a fine, upstanding woman. She doesn't deserve to be trifled with by someone of less than honorable intentions.

MARTIN: At least I have intentions, Sam. And I don't hide them, either. It's probably refreshing for her to have a man show honest interest for a change.

SAM: Honest interest? Really! Did you tell her you were married?

MARTIN: [*grins*] The topic never came up.

SAM: Right. [*rises to his feet*] Dane, please forgive me, but I think it best if I made an early exit this evening.

DANE: Sam, he–

SAM: Please excuse me.

[SAM *strides out the door.*]

DANE: [*frustrated*] Martin, was that really necessary?

MARTIN: Yes, I believe it was.

EMILE: Dude, how could that be necessary?

MARTIN: [*puts his index finger to his mouth*] Shhh, the grown-ups are talking.

EMILE: You know, I was looking forward to coming here, tonight. After last week, I thought, hey, this is kind of cool. Hanging out with you guys, talking about the book and life and stuff. But, tonight, you're kind of ruining it, dude. Sam's the nicest guy in here, and you just ran him off.

MARTIN: That's precisely his problem. He's the nicest guy here. And nice guys don't win the girls.

EMILE: Yeah, well...it doesn't sound like assistant librarians do so hot, either.

MARTIN: [*laughs*] Oh, nicely done! I know one woman, in particular, who would agree with you.

EMILE: [*to* DANE] Um, not that this isn't fun and all, but I think I'm going to head out, too, man.

DANE: I'm sorry, Emile. Let's try again, next week.

EMILE: [*stands-up*] No worries. I'll be here. [*to* MARTIN] Dude, I like you better when you're sober.

MARTIN: That's funny, because I like you better when I'm not.

EMILE: Whatever, man.

RETT: Have a good night, Emile.

EMILE: Later.

    [EMILE *exits.*]

RETT: [*to* DANE] You think Sam will come back after that?

DANE: I hope so. I'll call him at his office this week and talk to him.

MARTIN: Oh, he'll be back. I bet he'll spend the next week preparing a speech on marital propriety, just for me.

DANE: What was all that between you two, tonight?

MARTIN: Oh, it's nothing. Just having a little fun, is all. He'll be fine.

    [*A pause.* DANE *glances at* RETT *then back at* MARTIN.]

DANE: Well, Martin…look, I want you to come back next week, OK?

MARTIN: Of course. I'll clear my social calendar.

DANE: But here's the thing: I want you to come back sober.

    [MARTIN *gasps.*]

DANE: And if you can't do that, I think it would be better if you didn't come.

MARTIN: [*looks to* RETT] And what does our ex-pastor think?

RETT: He's the boss, Martin. I think you'd better listen to him.

MARTIN: And I thought God was the boss of our little arrangement, here. You said I was here by divine appointment.

RETT: That could be, Martin. But if there's a reason he wanted you here, then you have to make the most of it. You need to take it seriously.

MARTIN: There's no fun in taking things seriously. Those two are mutually exclusive.

DANE: Martin, in all seriousness, let me ask you something.

MARTIN: Uh-oh. The fun meter just dropped to zero.

DANE: What's the one thing that you think will make you happy?

MARTIN: Peanut butter. [*giggles to himself*]

DANE: Honestly, Martin, come on. What do you think would make you happy?

[*A pause*]

MARTIN: OK. You know what would make me happy? It would make me happy if my wife asked me that same question. "Martin, dear, what would make you happy?" Then I would at least know she had some interest and maybe even try and do something about it.

DANE: Martin, I'm going to share something with you I had to learn the hard way. You've got to make yourself happy.

MARTIN: I do. That's why I drink. [*grins*]

[DANE *drops his head in frustration.*]

RETT: I think what Dane meant, Martin, is that you can't rely on someone else to make you happy. If you do, you're always going to be disappointed. And I think that's where you are now.

MARTIN: But I'm justifiably disappointed, aren't I? Marriage is supposed to be about two people making each other happy. Isn't that what romance is all about?

DANE: And how is that expectation working out for you, so far?

MARTIN: It's not my expectation that's wrong; I just chose unwisely, that's all.

DANE: And you think drinking and seeing another woman is going to fix that? That's not how you find happiness in life, Martin.

MARTIN: I suppose you're going to tell me that Jesus is the answer to all my problems. That I should just give him a try, and he'll make me happy.

DANE: Jesus isn't something you try, Martin. You either know him, or you don't. And if you do, it will change your life. He offers something better than happiness.

MARTIN: Well, what if I don't want to change? What if I like the way I am?

DANE: Rett, we've seen Martin four weeks in a row, now, haven't we?

RETT: Yep.

DANE: Have you seen anything that tells you he likes his life the way it is?

RETT: [chuckles lightly] To the contrary, Dane. I'd say Martin is self-medicating his way through a painful, meaningless existence and an unhappy marriage.

MARTIN: Good god, man! Way to pile on!

DANE: We're not trying to gang-up on you, Martin. We're trying to help you.

MARTIN: [stands to his feet, wobbles] Well, gentlemen, I think that's all the help I need for tonight. I think I'll go home and spend a quiet evening sitting in a corner watching my wife knit. [giggles]

DANE: Hang-on, Martin. Rett, I'm going to drive Martin home in his car. Will you follow me and bring me back here?

RETT: Sure.

MARTIN: You can't drive me home; you don't know where I live.

DANE: Do you know where you live?

MARTIN: Of course, I know – oh, that's right. I'll be in the car with you. I'll tell you how to get there.

DANE: There you go.

MARTIN: Sorry.

DANE: Next week, Martin: Sober. Promise?

MARTIN: [*stands straight and raises an eyebrow*] "It is not the oath that makes us believe the man, but the man the oath." Aeschylus, 500 BC.

   [RETT *rolls his eyes.*]

DANE: Then make sure the man is sober next week. [*holds out his hand to* MARTIN] Car keys?

MARTIN: I'm perfectly capable of driving myself, you know.

DANE: Keys?

MARTIN: [*digs his keys from his pocket and drops them in* DANE's *hand*] Fine. [*meanders out the door*]

RETT: Interesting little study group you have here, Dane.

DANE: Isn't it?

   [RETT *and* DANE *exit.*]

Curtain

ACT TWO

Scene Two

DANE *enters the empty classroom, turns on the lights and begins the weekly task of arranging chairs. He takes a seat in the lone chair facing the semi-circle before him. He flips through the pages of his notebook as he waits for others to arrive. After a moment,* RETT *enters carrying a cup of Starbucks coffee and his copy of the book.*

RETT: Hey, Dane. Did you run everyone off?

DANE: Hey, Rett. It may just be you and me, tonight.

RETT: Why? Did you hear from everyone? [*tosses his book on a chair and sits down next to it at the end of the row*]

DANE: No. But I left a message for Sam at his office this morning, and I didn't hear back from him. I know he was fed-up with Martin last week. And Emile was, too, for the way he talked to Sam. So, I don't know if they'll show or not.

RETT: Dane, in my experience, [*leans back in his chair and crosses his legs as* DANE *lets out a sigh*] a lot of these groups peter-out after a few weeks. It happens even to the best of us. Don't take it personally.

DANE: Well, it's a little hard not to.

RETT: Maybe they've just lost interest in the book. You never know.

DANE: But I chose the book; I'm leading the discussion. If it fails, who else can I blame?

RETT: Group dynamics have a life of their own, Dane. You mix the wrong ingredients, you get a bad cake. It doesn't matter who puts it in the oven, so to speak.

DANE: Well, I think my cake might have a bad apple in it.

RETT: [*chuckles*] You think he'll show this week?

DANE: [*shrugs*] No idea. He was surprisingly quiet on the drive home last week. I couldn't get anything out of him.

RETT: That's not like him.

DANE: No, it's not. I guess he prefers a larger audience. I was kind of hoping I would get to meet his wife, though.

RETT: He made sure that didn't happen, making you get out like that.

DANE: Actually, he asked me very nicely. He didn't want her to see him being driven home by someone. And I was pretty sure he could drive one block without doing any damage, so....

RETT: I wonder what she looks like.

DANE: Martin's wife?

RETT: Yeah. In my imagination, I see some large, cold fish with her hair in a bun and a deep voice. And she wears pantsuits.

[DANE *laughs.*]

[MARTIN *enters.*]

[DANE *stops laughing.*]

MARTIN: She's actually very pretty.

RETT: [*startled and embarrassed*] Martin, I was just...we were just....

MARTIN: [*takes a seat opposite* RETT *on the other end of the row*] Stylishly delicate, too. If you saw her, you'd probably say she's a bit on the thin side. But I prefer the waifish Audrey Hepburn type.

DANE: We were just saying how disappointed we were not to get to meet her last week. Weren't we, Rett?

[RETT *nods in agreement.*]

MARTIN: You know, the funny thing about being attracted to a skinny woman is that, while I love how she looks, I can't help wanting to feed her. You know, take her to Waffle House and just shove an All Star in front of her. Which totally works against my attraction to her in the first place. It's very conflicting. [*offers a warm grin to* RETT]

RETT: Martin, it's good to see you.

MARTIN: Sober, you mean. [*looks to* DANE] That was our deal, wasn't it?

DANE: Yes, it was. I just wasn't sure which way you'd go on that.

MARTIN: Well, I wasn't either. But your book seems to be holding my interest. I have to see how our dynamic duo fare on their trip. Does Jon get the girl? Does he get his job back? I couldn't miss out on our riveting conversations about all that, could I?

DANE: Well, I'm glad you're enjoying it.

MARTIN: Do you know if Sam is coming?

DANE: I'm not sure.

[EMILE *enters.*]

EMILE: Hey.

DANE: Hey, Emile. How's it going?

EMILE: [*takes a seat next to* RETT] I'm good. It's been a long day, though. Where's Sam? He's usually here by now.

DANE: I'm not sure he's coming. I tried to reach him but didn't get a call back.

EMILE: Well, I'm not sure I'd blame him if he didn't come. [*gives a nod to* MARTIN] What's up, Martin?

MARTIN: Greetings.

EMILE: [*to* MARTIN] So like, which Martin do we get this week, dude?

MARTIN: The chemically unaltered one.

EMILE: Oh, cool. That's an improvement.

MARTIN: That's a matter of one's perspective. I'm curious, you said you've had a long day. I didn't know the life of leisure could be so rigorous.

EMILE: I stay busy, man. Just 'cause I don't have a job doesn't mean I don't do stuff.

MARTIN: And what stuff did you do today?

EMILE: Well, I got up.

MARTIN: Was that before or after noon?

EMILE: Before...kind of. But then I had to take my mom shopping. And she likes to go to the flea markets, even though I tell her we can afford to go to a real mall and buy real stuff. You know, new things instead of the junk you find at the flea market. But we didn't just go to one flea market; we went to three flea markets. Walking all over, up and down. And the thing is, the only thing she bought all day was an old ceramic cookie jar shaped like a monk with the words "Thou shalt not steal" painted on it. She thought it was a sign from God. I'm telling you, man, it was a long day.

MARTIN: OK, I believe you, now. Thank you.

[SAM *enters cautiously.*]

EMILE: Sam! I was just asking if you were coming, man!

SAM: Yes, I do apologize for being late. Bit of an emergency at my office.

[SAM *sits between* EMILE *and* MARTIN.]

MARTIN: Couldn't find the pliers, again?

SAM: No. A client's Weimaraner had eaten a KitKat.

EMILE: A dog ate a cat?

SAM: No, the candy bar. He'd swallowed chocolate. Very toxic for dogs, you know.

EMILE: Oh, so like, is this going to be one of your pet enema stories?

MARTIN: Other end, Emile.

SAM: Exactly, Martin. Induced vomiting is the prescription for ingested chocolate. A few tablespoons of hydrogen peroxide syringed down his throat and he chundered right up. Left an awful mess for my assistant to clean up, though. I feel rather bad about that, but I had to leave to come here.

EMILE: Dude, cat enemas and dog puke. I'm glad I don't have your job.

MARTIN: You mean, a job.

EMILE: Well....

SAM: Martin, I see you're relatively unaffected this evening.

MARTIN: That may be the most polite way of saying, "Martin, I see you're not stinking drunk this evening" that I've ever heard.

SAM: Well, I must say I'm relieved. You were quite the handful last week.

MARTIN: [smiles at SAM] Isn't there something you're dying to ask me, Sam.

SAM: No, I don't believe there is.

MARTIN: You're not even the least bit interested to know how my date with Ms. Hannah Walker went, Saturday?

SAM: Martin, I assure you, the details of your nefarious rendezvous with a sweet, unsuspecting girl is none of my concern. I'd rather pretend it never happened.

MARTIN: She talked about you.

SAM: She did? What did she say?

MARTIN: Ah-ha! You are interested!

SAM: Well, I suppose…only if it pertains to me directly. Otherwise, please keep the rest of your sordid evening to yourself.

MARTIN: To be honest, our whole evening pertained to you.

SAM: [*surprised*] How is that?

MARTIN: Well, you see, she seems to have this insatiable crush on a certain veterinarian.

SAM: It's not Dr. Varnon is it? I lose more patients to that man.

MARTIN: [*laughs*] It's you, Sam! For heaven's sake!

SAM: Me? Are you sure? Because Dr. Varnon is a very handsome man. A bit aloof, or so I've heard, but very well thought of. I wouldn't be a bit surprised if–

MARTIN: Sam, listen to me! I'm embarrassed to admit it, but you're all she talked about. Here I am paying for her drink, which she hardly touched, having to listen to her go on and on about what a kind, gentle, wonderful man you are. It was humiliating. Not to mention a waste of perfectly good gin.

DANE: Wow. What do you say to that, Sam?

SAM: Well, I don't know…I'm not quite sure what it all means.

EMILE: Dude, it means you should ask her out.

SAM: On a date, you mean?

EMILE: Yeah, like movies, popcorn, that sort of thing.

MARTIN: Thanks for reminding us why you're still single, Emile. Sam, forget about movies and popcorn. Take her to a romantic dinner somewhere. Wine and dine her.

SAM: [*nods in thought*] Wine and dine, yes….

MARTIN: But look, you can't mention anything about me. I can't have her finding out I'm married.

SAM: Right, not a word.

MARTIN: [*sits back and smiles*] So, are you going to do it?

SAM: Do what, exactly?

MARTIN: Ask her out! Take her to dinner! Romance, Sam, romance!

SAM: Oh, yes. Well… [*seriously*] I promise to give it my utmost consideration, Martin. Mustn't be too rash about these sorts of things, you know. No. It'll take some planning. Not scheming, mind you. Just deliberate forethought. I'll definitely have to make time for it.

MARTIN: [*sighs and looks at* SAM] "It is not time or opportunity that is to determine intimacy; it is disposition alone."

DANE: Jane Austen? *Sense and Sensibility*?

MARTIN: An A for the English lit teacher.

DANE: [*chuckles*] OK, guys, well, on that literary note, what did you think of our book from this past week? The story shifted gears a bit. Any surprises, likes or dislikes?

EMILE: Well, I kinda want to go back to what Sam said last week about how Jon kind of disses Lacey sometimes. That chapter where he brings home a Bible instead of diapers–

MARTIN: My least favorite chapter in the book, so far. Totally pointless. Unless the author just wanted to paint his protagonist as having the emotional intelligence of a doorknob.

EMILE: Yeah, but still, I don't think she had to rail on him like that. I mean, the guy was trying to be nice. He brought her a gift.

MARTIN: Said the naïve single man.

RETT: Emile, I think the author wants us to see Jon's timing in talking with Lacey about his faith as being very shortsighted and somewhat self-motivated. Being the only one among us who's experienced the joy of having a newborn in the house, I can safely say that it's not uncommon for a new mother to be very emotional at times. The wise husband is very sensitive to that fact and would avoid topics or issues that may upset his wife unnecessarily.

MARTIN: [*chuckles*] The wise husband...you mean the one who lives in Oz and rides a unicorn? There's no such thing, in all practicality. Being a husband is like walking across a minefield blindfolded. Wisdom counts for nothing.

RETT: I'm not saying it's easy, Martin. It takes care, hard work and a loving attitude. But it's not impossible to be a wise and successful husband.

MARTIN: I guess I'd have to see one to believe you.

DANE: Hey, Rett, here's an idea: Maybe you could help Martin see what you're talking about.

RETT: How would I do that?

DANE: Well, what if you and Camille met Martin and his wife out for dinner sometime? You know, spend some time together as couples. Maybe then he could see how you are with your wife.

RETT: Uh, well, Dane....

MARTIN: [*to* DANE] How nice of you to offer on his behalf. He's clearly eager to take you up on it.

RETT: It's not that I wouldn't, Martin. It's just that....

DANE: [*to* RETT] I could babysit, if that's what you're worried about.

RETT: Thank you, Dane. But....

DANE: But what?

MARTIN: [*to* DANE] Oh, let the poor man off the hook. After all, it's easier to talk about helping people than actually doing it, isn't it, Pastor?

RETT: Now, just a minute, Martin. I'd be happy to help you, if I could. But the fact is...my wife is in Louisiana.

DANE: OK, so just plan something when she gets back. How long is she gone for, Rett?

[*A pause*]

RETT: [*slowly*] She's not actually gone, per se.

DANE: What do you mean?

[*A pause*]

RETT: She never left Brouillette.

DANE: She didn't come with you to South Carolina? But you've been here for months.

RETT: I know.

DANE: I'm confused. You mean you moved here without your...but you said....

RETT: I never said they were here with me. You just assumed that.

DANE: Well, why wouldn't I?

MARTIN: [*to* RETT] Was that your unicorn tied up outside?

DANE: [*shakes his head*] Martin.

MARTIN: [*to* DANE] I'm not trying to take joy in his problems – whatever they are – but he proves my point. Even pastors – or ex-pastors in this case – the flag bearers of wisdom, find marriage tough sledding. The only difference between him and me is that I admit being a failure at it.

RETT: I'm not a failure at being a husband, Martin. Camille and I are...we're just trying to sort some things out, right now.

DANE: But Rett, you have a baby girl and three other daughters. What happened? Why did you come here without them?

RETT: [*shifts uncomfortably in his seat*] I told you, Dane, I'm on a new spiritual journey, so to speak, and I believe the Lord has something in store for me, a new opportunity, perhaps. A chance to….

DANE: A chance to what?

RETT: Well, it's not unlike the characters in our book, here. Brant and Jon both see an opportunity to find real meaning and purpose in their faith. And to do that, they had to make some changes. Get out of their comfort zone and trust in the Lord's direction. And look what happened? God used them to reach those two girls in Charleston.

MARTIN: Two fictional girls, you mean.

DANE: Martin, when I met this author, he told me that he based a lot of his characters on real encounters he's had with people. Who's to say the story of Tiffany and Megan didn't really happen?

SAM: I do have a question about that, if I may.

DANE: Sure, Sam. Go ahead.

SAM: Right. Here goes. It's always been my presumption, my understanding – which may be off, mind you – that people who consider themselves Christian were simply brought up that way. Trained in the faith by their schooling or parental teaching.

DANE: In many cases that's true, Sam. What's your question?

SAM: Well, then I'm a little confused as to what Jon's mission is. Is he trying to find people who are Christians but have strayed from their beliefs, as seemed to be the case with Tiffany and Megan? I seem to recall he did say he was looking for lost sheep, which leads me to assume that the sheep he's looking for were once in the pen, as it were. Or, rather, does he hope to find non-Christians and somehow convince them to be Christians, which is what I thought he was intending to do?

MARTIN: Whether they're fake Christians or my fellow members of the great unwashed makes no difference, whatsoever. I would think his mission is the same.

DANE: OK, anyone have any thoughts about that? Rett?

[RETT *remains silent.*]

EMILE: Well, I'm kind of new to the whole non-Catholic Christianity thing, so I was kind of wondering about all that. I mean, Jon made it seem pretty simple to be a Christian when he was talking to those two girls. They just prayed for a paragraph and boom, they're in. My mom's always made it seem like a lot of hard work.

DANE: Well, Emile, first, let me ask: Who do you think meets the definition of a Christian?

EMILE: Um, you want me to say Jesus, right?

MARTIN: [*laughs*] Always the safe answer in church, but no. Jesus was a Jew, not a Christian.

EMILE: All right, well, who then, smart guy?

MARTIN: Well, certainly not me, that's all I know.

DANE: Let me ask it a different way. What is the definition of a Christian?

[*A slight pause*]

MARTIN: I'm sorry, but there's a fallacy in the question.

DANE: How so?

MARTIN: As it's phrased, it assumes only one right answer.

DANE: That's right, it does. But I don't see that as a flaw, Martin. It's intentional.

MARTIN: But that's like asking someone to define ice cream. Do you mean Chunky Monkey or Oreo? Vanilla or chocolate? Strawberry or peach? Extra creamy or lactose-free? And then there's the whole question of gelato. [*observes* EMILE *staring blankly ahead*] You all right, over there?

EMILE: Huh? Yeah. I was just thinking.

MARTIN: About ice cream or Christianity?

DANE: Martin, I'll give you that there are different denominations, or flavors, within Christianity, but from what you've read so far in our book, how do you think the definition of being a Christian is presented? How does the author put it in Biblical terms?

RETT: Dane, if I could interject for a moment.

DANE: Sure, Rett.

MARTIN: [*in a subdued, serious tone*] And now, our sermon from Dr. McCasguill.

RETT: [*ignores* MARTIN] I was just going to say that I certainly see Martin's point.

DANE: You can?

MARTIN: You can?

RETT: Yes. And, in a practical sense, he's correct.

MARTIN: Again? Score another point for the librarian!

RETT: You're right, Martin, but what you said isn't something to be excited about. In many circles within the Church, what it means to be a Christian has been watered-down and altered to mean something other than what the Bible defines for us. I think that's part of what Jon's challenge is going to be in our book. In the chapter where they talked with the girls in Charleston, Jon relied on Romans 10:9-10 to help them understand what it means to commit in faith to Christ. That worked for them, but I doubt you can use the same approach with everyone. Not that the definition is different but because people are different. They're all coming at the same question from different angles and preconceived notions. You see that in how Jesus responded to people in the Gospels. He didn't address any two people the same way but still led them in the same direction.

[JUDITH *walks past the doorway, stops, looks in and sees* MARTIN.]

JUDITH: Marty?

MARTIN: [*startled*] Judith!

DANE: [*to* MARTIN] Marty?

JUDITH: [*takes a small step into the room*] Is this the AA meeting?

MARTIN: Um.... [*stands to approach* JUDITH *but takes a quick look back at* DANE] Yes, it is. What are you doing here?

JUDITH: I wanted to see where it was you were going every week. You said if I didn't believe you, I should come see for myself.

MARTIN: That was intended to make you believe me, not follow me.

JUDITH: [*looks around the room*] I thought it would be a much bigger group than this.

MARTIN: Well, they must be running out of alcoholics. I'll see you when I get home. [*turns* JUDITH*'s shoulders toward the door*]

DANE: Martin, you're not going to introduce us?

MARTIN: [*turns slowly to face the group*] Gentlemen, this is my wife, Judith. Judith, this is my...group.

DANE: [*stands*] Hello, Judith. It's nice to meet you. [*shakes her hand*] I'm Dane. And this is Rett, Sam and Emile.

[*All three men stand and offer a collective scattering of hellos.*]

MARTIN: She just came to check-up on me, apparently. [*looks at* JUDITH]

JUDITH: Actually, I was driving past the church on the way home and saw our minivan in the parking lot. So, I turned in. Is it OK if I stay for a few minutes?

101

MARTIN: Well, it is a group for men, only. And besides, you're not an alcoholic.

JUDITH: Oh. Well. [*glances around, unsure*]

DANE: Martin, I think we can make an exception for Judith, since she's already here. Just this once. [*winks at* MARTIN]

MARTIN: [*cautiously*] Well, all right, if you think it's OK. But it has to be OK with everyone else. [*takes a step back, out of view from* JUDITH, *and shakes his head instructively*]

EMILE: [*ignores* MARTIN's *prompt and hurriedly retrieves a chair, unfolds it and places it on the end of the row next to* MARTIN's] Here's a chair.

[MARTIN *drops his head in defeat.*]

EMILE: You can sit here.

JUDITH: Thank you. [*sits down*]

EMILE: Emile. [*smiles*]

JUDITH: Thank you, Emile.

[*All five men retake their seats.*]

DANE: Judith, if it's OK, we'll just pick back up where we were in our discussion.

JUDITH: Oh, that's fine. Just pretend I'm not here.

MARTIN: That was a lot easier to do a few minutes ago.

DANE: So, Sam?

SAM: Yes?

DANE: You were about to tell us how long it's been since you've had a drink.

SAM: I was?

DANE: Yes. You've been sober for how many months, now?

SAM: Uh…well, I really can't say, actually.

DANE: So long that you can't remember. That's excellent. Let's give Sam a hand, guys.

[DANE, MARTIN *and* JUDITH *clap lightly.*]

EMILE: Oh, I get it. [*raises his hand*] Can I go next?

DANE: Sure, Emile. What would you like to share?

EMILE: [*to* JUDITH] Well, I used to drink, see? A lot. You know, like, all the time. Because…I'm an alcoholic. But then I joined this kind of book club thing and met this cool group of guys. And they helped me see what an obnoxious, sarcastic–

MARTIN: That's good, Emile. Thank you for sharing.

JUDITH: No, Marty, let him finish. I'm interested. Go ahead….

EMILE: Emile. [*smiles*]

JUDITH: Yes, go ahead, Emile.

EMILE: I was just saying that they helped me see how rude and stuff I was when I drank and how much nicer, sort of, I was when I didn't. Drink, I mean.

DANE: [*smiles*] That's very inspiring, Emile. Thank you. Sometimes we need other people to help us see ourselves differently, don't we? Rett, do you have anything you'd like to share with the group?

RETT: Dane, I think it's disingenuous for us to pretend to be something we're not.

MARTIN: [*laughs deliberately*] That's so true, isn't it? And that's what happens when we drink; we pretend to be something we're not. An excellent point, Dr. McCasguill. [*to* JUDITH] He's an ex-pastor.

JUDITH: Oh.

MARTIN: Dane, isn't it about time for us to wrap-up? [*taps the face of his wrist watch*]

DANE: Sure, I suppose we can stop there. Judith, I'm glad we got to meet you. Martin's told us so much about you.

JUDITH: He has? That's a bit scary to think about. What did he say? [*looks at* MARTIN]

DANE: Oh. Well, only that he... [*looks at* MARTIN *then back to* JUDITH] wants to make you happy. And just tonight, he was saying how pretty and stylish and attractive you are. I think he compared you to Katharine Hepburn.

RETT: Audrey Hepburn, Dane.

MARTIN: Yes. Big difference.

JUDITH: Oh, I love Audrey Hepburn. [*looks at* MARTIN] Did you really say all that, Marty?

MARTIN: Yes, I did. My words, exactly. Now, we really should be going. [*stands and offers his hand to* JUDITH]

[JUDITH *stands.*]

[DANE *stands.*]

MARTIN: [*to* JUDITH] Let's go get you something to eat. How does Waffle House sound?

JUDITH: Oh, no. They don't have good salads there.

[MARTIN *sighs.*]

DANE: Judith, we're glad you came to visit, tonight. Martin's shown a lot of progress over the last few weeks. We're glad to have him in our group.

JUDITH: Oh, well, thank you. That's very nice to hear. I'll make sure he keeps coming.

MARTIN: Yes, thank you, Dane. I'll see you next week.

DANE: Sounds good. See you then.

[MARTIN *and* JUDITH *exit.*]

[DANE *retakes his seat.*]

RETT: [*waits for a moment as he watches the door*] Do you really think that was a good idea, Dane? Pretending we're an AA group?

SAM: Oh, I see, now. We were pretending. Yes, of course! Can I have a go at it?

EMILE: Dude, they're gone.

DANE: Rett, would you rather have Martin exposed as a liar to his wife in front of all of us? We'd never see him again. Besides, I didn't say we were an AA group.

RETT: Well, you certainly gave her that impression. I just don't think it's right to put on false airs, that's all.

DANE: I was just trying to help the guy out.

EMILE: I thought Judith was pretty nice.

DANE: She didn't seem like the cold-hearted monster he'd made her out to be, did she?

SAM: I found her most pleasant, actually. They make a rather handsome couple, the two of them. It makes me wonder why Martin would want to pursue another woman. It just doesn't make sense to me. But then, I'm certainly not the expert in that arena, now, am I?

EMILE: Did she really say Martin drives a minivan?

DANE: He does. I drove him home in it last week.

EMILE: Why would anyone own a minivan when they don't have to? He doesn't have any kids, does he?

DANE: He hasn't mentioned any.

RETT: [*looks at his watch*] I should be going.

DANE: OK, well, sorry we got off topic tonight, guys. But we'll pick it up again, next week. Rett, do you want to go grab some coffee or something?

RETT: I can't tonight, Dane. I have a…uh…a few things I need to take care of. Maybe next time.

DANE: No worries. I'll pray for us real quick and you can be off.

EMILE: I don't drink coffee, but is anyone up for some ice cream or gelato?

[SAM *raises his hand.*]

EMILE: Awesome!

DANE: Let's pray.

[*The group bows their heads to pray and the curtain closes.*]

Curtain

ACT TWO

Scene Three

MARTIN *staggers into the dark, empty classroom and stumbles over a chair, catching himself before falling. He takes a seat in the chair and sits quietly in the dark.* DANE *enters a moment later and turns on the lights.* MARTIN *shields his eyes and hisses like a vampire exposed to the sun.*

DANE: Martin! Why are you sitting in here in the…. [*stops, studies* MARTIN *for a moment*] Aww, man…you've been drinking, again.

MARTIN: [*nods*] So it would appear.

DANE: [*moves into the room*] Martin, I thought we had a deal.

MARTIN: As I recall, good teacher, our deal was that I come sober last week, which I did. You didn't say anything about this week or any other week. A rather shocking oversight on your part; you have to admit.

DANE: [*sets his book and notebook down on a chair and sits in the chair next to it facing* MARTIN] Martin, what am I going to do with you?

MARTIN: Hmm, that sounds vaguely familiar. You must be channeling your inner-Judith.

DANE: I just don't understand why you'd want to come here like this.

MARTIN: It was totally seren…serendip…. [*holds up his index finger*] I'll get it in a moment…serendipitous. There. Your study group just happened to fall on the same night The Crescent Moon had a happy hour special on Tanqueray and tonic. Who am I to argue with fate?

[EMILE *enters and stops just inside the doorway upon seeing* MARTIN *slumped in his chair.*]

EMILE: Oh, dude. This doesn't look good.

DANE: Hey, Emile. Martin, do you want me to take you home?

MARTIN: [*straightens himself in his chair*] No. I'm here, and I intend to be an active participant in our discussion of one man's meager attempt to save the world. Our hero, Jon Smoak.

DANE: Emile, would you mind arranging the chairs for us while I talk with Martin?

EMILE: Sure, no sweat. [*begins folding the extra chairs and leaning them against the wall*]

DANE: Martin, I covered for you last week when Judith was here, but–

MARTIN: Yes, you did. That was quite a performance, too. She thinks I'm in a wonderful recovery group. [*giggles*]

DANE: Yeah, but now I'm wondering if I did the right thing. You really do need help, Martin. And I'm not sure my group is where you need to be. I can't be responsible for–

MARTIN: Oh, stop. Just let me stay, and I'll make whatever empty promises you need to ease your conscience.

DANE: That's not very reassuring.

MARTIN: It will have to do for the moment.

[EMILE *finishes the task of arranging chairs around* MARTIN *and sits down on the end of the row.*]

EMILE: Dude, what's your wife gonna say when you come home like this?

MARTIN: It won't matter. I have the exceeding ability to forget anything I don't want to hear. For example, what did you just ask me?

EMILE: I said–

DANE: Emile. [*shakes his head at* EMILE]

[MARTIN *giggles.*]

EMILE: Oh.

MARTIN: I tell you what; I have an idea. [*begins to slide off his chair onto his knees*] While we wait for the others to show, I'm just going to take a little nap, right here. [*rolls onto his back in the middle of the floor and closes his eyes*] Wake me up if Sam tells any good cat stories.

[*A pause as* DANE *and* EMILE *sit staring at* MARTIN *on the floor*]

EMILE: [*to* DANE] Dude, seriously?

[SAM *enters and stops, seeing* MARTIN *on the floor.*]

SAM: Oh, my. Is he…?

DANE: No, Sam, he's not dead. He's just passed out; he drank too much.

SAM: [*takes a seat next to* EMILE] How long has he been like this?

DANE: He just sprawled out right before you walked in. He said he was taking a nap until everyone got here.

SAM: Hmm. You know, I had an uncle growing up who had a problem with alcohol, much like our friend Martin, here. Uncle Benedict. He used to go off on long benders, sometimes lasting for days. Then we'd find him asleep in the most unusual places. My mother once borrowed his car to drive to the market, and when she opened the boot, she found him balled-up asleep inside.

EMILE: What did she do?

SAM: She just set her groceries down next to him, closed the lid and drove home. When she opened it up again, there he was: awake and eating from a bag of dog treats.

[RETT *enters casually, holding a Starbucks cup, undeterred by the sight of* MARTIN *on the floor.*]

RETT: Evening, gentlemen! [*steps over* MARTIN *and takes a seat opposite* EMILE]

DANE: Hey, Rett.

RETT: [*looks down at* MARTIN] What do we have here?

DANE: Martin's taking a nap.

EMILE: He's drunk.

RETT: Thank you, Emile, but I surmised that on my own.

EMILE: Well, you asked.

RETT: [*to* DANE] Was he like this when you got here?

DANE: No, we talked for a moment. Then he just.... [*waves his hand toward* MARTIN]

EMILE: What do you guys think we should do with him?

DANE: Well, I suppose there's no harm in letting him lay there while we talk. He's not hurting anyone. Would that be all right with you guys?

RETT: Fine by me.

SAM: I surely don't mind.

EMILE: Might be a nice change.

DANE: OK, then, let's get started. [*moves his notebook onto his lap and opens it*] How was everyone's week? Anything interesting happen?

EMILE: You mean besides seeing a drunk guy pass out on the floor at church?

DANE: Yes, besides the obvious.

[SAM *raises his hand.*]

DANE: Yes, Sam.

SAM: Well, since we last talked, I've had a rather interesting conversation with my client Ms. Walker.

EMILE: That cat chick who's got the hots for you?

SAM: Uh....

RETT: The woman you and Martin talked about last week? Hannah, was it?

SAM: Yes, Hannah. She came by my office unexpectedly on Monday but without Major Tom.

EMILE: Who's Major Tom?

SAM: Her cat.

EMILE: Oh. She's a David Bowie fan.

[SAM *stares blankly at* EMILE.]

EMILE: You know, "ground control to Major Tom," blah, blah, blah....

SAM: [*nods*] Ah, right, yes.

EMILE: You have no idea what I'm talking about, do you?

SAM: No, I'm afraid not.

DANE: Go ahead with your story, Sam.

SAM: Yes, well, she – Ms. Walker – waited several minutes, which I felt bad about later because I didn't know she was there. I was checking a puppy for worms and–

EMILE: Dude, please spare us the details on that one.

SAM: Surely. So, once my assistant let me know she was waiting, I washed my hands and stepped out to see her. And, I must say, I was a bit startled by her appearance.

RETT: Why? How'd she look?

SAM: Rather stunning, actually. I'd only seen her in gym clothes previously, as that's what she wears when she brings in Major Tom. But on this occasion, she wore a black dress. And her hair had been fashioned in a way I hadn't seen before. I thought perhaps I should ask if she were on her way to attend a funeral.

111

DANE: You didn't ask her that, did you?

SAM: No. Before I could say anything, she told me she had come to ask me a question.

DANE: What was it?

SAM: Well, there's a rather large fundraising event for homeless pets coming up. It's quite the formal affair every year. Tuxedos, evening gowns, music, food and drink.

DANE: The Fur Ball.

SAM: Precisely.

DANE: I've been to that before. It's a big deal.

SAM: Yes, it is. And Ms. Walker asked if I knew about it. Of course, I did, you know. We have an event poster right there in our lobby. I donate what I can each year, but it's never as much as I would like. It's a sad thing, homeless pets. I end up treating a lot of them. Just last week–

DANE: Sam.

SAM: Oh, sorry.

DANE: Did she ask you to go with her to the fundraiser?

SAM: No, that's the interesting thing, you see. She said she was hoping to go, but she didn't want to go alone. I told her I could sympathize, as I was going alone as well.

EMILE: [*shakes his head*] Dude.

SAM: [*reads the faces around the room*] Should I not have told her I was going? She did seem a bit bothered by it. Maybe she doesn't want me there.

EMILE: [*to* DANE] Should we wake-up Martin? He might want to hear all this.

DANE: No. What happened next, Sam?

SAM: She left.

MARTIN: [*without moving or opening his eyes*] Sam, you're an idiot.

DANE: Martin, you're awake.

MARTIN: No, I'm not.

EMILE: Dude, you're just lying there listening to us talk? That's kind of rude, man.

MARTIN: [*eyes still closed*] Have you met me, Emile?

DANE: Martin, would you like to sit in a chair and join us? Or are you just going to lie there on the floor all night?

[MARTIN *begins to roll himself over.*]

EMILE: Look, it's moving.

[DANE *and* RETT *laugh.*]

MARTIN: A joke from the elephant in the room. [*gets to his knees, crawls to his chair and pulls himself up into a sitting position*] Now, Sam. Here's what you're going to do. Tomorrow morning, you're going to call Hannah.

SAM: I am?

MARTIN: Yes. You're going to call her and ask her if she would like to go with you to the Hair Ball.

SAM: Fur Ball.

MARTIN: Same thing. Call her.

SAM: But how will I know if that's what she wants?

MARTIN: It's simple. You'll ask, and she'll answer. That's how these things work.

SAM: Ah. That really is simple, when you put it like that.

MARTIN: It's the beauty of talking to a woman on the phone. No non-verbals to throw you off or batting eyelashes to distract you.

SAM: Ah, yes. Excellent point.

MARTIN: And make sure you call her between ten and ten-thirty in the morning. That's when women are most receptive to social invitations.

SAM: [*pulls a small note pad and pen from his sport coat pocket and begins writing*] Between ten and ten-thirty. That's very instructive. Thank you.

EMILE: [*to* RETT] Is that true?

    [RETT *rolls his eyes and shakes his head.*]

MARTIN: [*to* SAM] And if you don't have the guts to ask her, I will.

SAM: That would be nice of you, Martin. I'll let you know.

MARTIN: With me, dog brain. I'll ask her to go with me, if you don't take her.

SAM: Oh. Well…. [*appears uncertain*]

DANE: [*leans forward*] Sam, would you like to go with Hannah to the Fur Ball?

SAM: Well, yes, I think that would be most exciting. But I—

DANE: Then ask her. From everything Martin's said about her, I'm sure she'll say yes.

SAM: [*glances at* MARTIN] Well, if it will keep her from going with a married man, I believe I must.

MARTIN: Make sure you tell her that's your motivation for asking. It'll sweep her off her feet.

    [SAM *writes in his notepad.*]

DANE: He's kidding, Sam.

SAM: [*scratches through his note*] Yes, of course.

DANE: OK, so let us know how it goes, Sam.

SAM: I certainly will. But the idea does make me a bit nervous.

DANE: You'll do fine. Anyone else have any news to share?

    [MARTIN *closes his eyes, lets his head drop back and mouth open wide.*]

DANE: All right, that's a *no* from Martin. Why don't we jump into the book, then? [*opens his notebook*] In our chapters for this week, we saw Brant and Jon have a few more encounters trying to share the Gospel. How did that go for them?

EMILE: Kind of all over the place. Good and bad.

DANE: A couple of hard conversations that didn't go so well and a couple of wins in there, too, right? What about the couple on the pier in Charleston that Brant talked to? They were pretty hostile to his message, weren't they? What did you think about that?

[MARTIN *straightens himself slightly in his chair.*]

RETT: Dane, it's not uncommon to find hostility towards the Gospel. That fact alone is enough to keep most Christians from sharing their faith. But we have to remind ourselves that some seeds fall on good soil; some fall on hard rock. It's our job to just keep casting.

MARTIN: [*opens his eyes*] So, I suppose in your analogy, I would be a hard rock. Is that true, ex-Pastor?

RETT: If your heart is hardened to the Gospel, Martin, then – metaphorically speaking – yes, that would apply to you.

MARTIN: Well, "the same sun that melts the wax, hardens the clay." Origen, *On First Principles,* third century.

RETT: Martin, anyone can toss out quotes. But wisdom belongs to the one being quoted.

MARTIN: Nice. Who said that?

DANE: Martin, are you saying it's God's fault your heart is hard towards him?

MARTIN: If God is sovereign and he causes everything, then why shouldn't I say that?

DANE: Do you blame him for your dinking?

MARTIN: To the contrary, for that I'm most appreciative.

RETT: Martin–

MARTIN: Excuse me. [*holds up his index finger*] I feel the need to be horizontal, again. [*slides off his chair onto his knees, then rolls onto his back and closes his eyes*]

DANE: That's good, Martin. Just take a nap. We'll wake you when it's time to leave.

[MARTIN *gives a faint wave of his hand.*]

DANE: Anyway, guys, in our book, the couple Brant approached didn't just have attitude problems. They had experienced real loss and suffering. Now, pretend you're Brant. How would you have handled that conversation?

EMILE: I don't know, man. Maybe you just don't bring up religion to people like that. I mean, who wants to get cussed at? I know I don't.

RETT: I would argue, Emile, that those people are the very ones who need to experience the love of Christ.

MARTIN: [*huffs from his place on the floor*] Those people. You wouldn't know what to say to those people if they were lying on the floor in front of you.

[*A slight pause*]

DANE: Are you saying you've experienced loss, Martin?

[*A slight pause*]

MARTIN: I have, yes.

DANE: Was it a parent or grandparent?

SAM: Or a pet, perhaps?

[*A slight pause*]

MARTIN: No. It was Emma.

RETT: [*chuckles*] Martin, I don't think a college girlfriend breaking up with you is the kind of pain and suffering we're talking about.

MARTIN: Not that Emma. My daughter, Emma.

EMILE: Dude, you named your daughter after your ex-girlfriend?

[*A slight pause*]

MARTIN: Emma was my wife's idea. She loved the name. Ironic, isn't it?

RETT: I didn't know you had a daughter, Martin.

MARTIN: Why do you think I drive a minivan?

EMILE: [*to* DANE] See?

DANE: [*ignores* EMILE] Did something...happen, Martin? To Emma?

[*A pause*]

MARTIN: One morning, last August [*pauses*] my wife found Emma in her crib. [*pauses*] Sudden infant death syndrome, they call it. As if that explains anything.

[*A pause*]

RETT: [*appears stunned, looks to* DANE *then to* MARTIN] Martin, I...don't know what to say.

MARTIN: That was my point. Now, if you'll excuse me, I think I'm going to sleep now.

[*A long pause as everyone watches* MARTIN *drift off to sleep*]

[RETT *lowers his head in thought and rests his elbows on his knees.*]

EMILE: [*quietly*] Whoa. That was heavy.

SAM: Yes. Poor fellow.

EMILE: No wonder he drinks so much.

DANE: You OK, Rett?

RETT: [*pushes himself upright*] I owe Martin an apology; I didn't see that coming. Sometimes these conversations don't go the way you expect them to.

EMILE: Yeah, kinda like that chapter in the book, where they talk to that protester kid, David, in the park.

DANE: That's a good example, Emile. I'm interested to know what you thought about that.

EMILE: Man, I thought it sucked. Not the chapter, just how it all worked out.

DANE: What about Jon's attempt to help David deal with the anger in his life? Any thoughts on that?

EMILE: Well, if you mean the whole absent dad thing, yeah...It kind of got to me, a little.

DANE: How so?

EMILE: Well, I know I said that if I could talk to my dad, I'd just tell him not to feel bad about leaving and all. Because I'm fine, I think. But...when I read that chapter in the book, I really felt for David. And I realized I might feel....

DANE: You think you might feel a little the same way?

EMILE: Yeah. Not that I want to go out protesting and cuss at people and stuff, but...it made me wonder if...maybe the reason I've always eaten like I do is because I'm mad at my dad or something like that. You know, psychology stuff.

DANE: You might be onto something, Emile. Maybe there's an emptiness inside you that's more than physical hunger. But food is just the quickest way to make yourself feel better. So you eat.

EMILE: But that sounds like Martin, only with food instead of alcohol. You think I'm a food-aholic?

DANE: Maybe. But let me ask you this: When you were reading about David, were you hoping he would make a decision in faith to accept Christ as his Savior?

EMILE: Yeah, I was. I really was. And I was a little miffed that he didn't. Brant had to argue with that other dude and mess everything up. [*to* RETT] And then they all went to your favorite coffee place, Doc.

RETT: [*lifts his cup with a smile and looks at* DANE] Starbucks.

DANE: Don't get me started. Emile, why did you want to see David saved?

EMILE: Well, because it seemed like what Jon was offering him was something better. A way to put what his dad did behind him and start fresh, you know. Without all the anger and protesting and stuff.

DANE: Would you like that for yourself, Emile?

EMILE: What?

DANE: A fresh start. A second chance from God, just like what Jon talked with David about.

[*A pause*]

EMILE: Yeah, but I don't know if I could ever do enough to deserve it. I'd have a lot of making up to do.

DANE: Emile, do you remember what you said to Martin when he was impressed with you for having money?

EMILE: Uh…I'm guessing I said something like, "Yeah, whatever, man."

DANE: No, I remember what you said. You said you didn't do anything to earn it. Your father did all the work. The only reason you got it was because he died.

EMILE: Yeah, that's right. I did say that.

DANE: Your inheritance was a gift. All you had to do was accept it, right?

EMILE: Yeah, so?

DANE: Emile, don't you see? It's exactly the same with God's love and forgiveness. You can't do anything to earn it. He did all the work for you. The only reason you can have it is because Jesus died for you. Your salvation is a gift, Emile. All you have to do is accept it.

EMILE: Wow. That's good stuff, man. That was just like Jon or Brant from the book.

DANE: Yes, but Emile, this isn't fiction. This is real life. And you can make that decision right here, right now, if you want.

EMILE: You mean like, decide to become a real Christian?

DANE: Once and for all. With no doubt and no strings attached.

[*A pause*]

RETT: What do you say, Emile?

EMILE: Don't I have to, like, join the church first or take a class?

RETT: Actually, you become a Christian first, then you join a church.

DANE: And there's no class or test.

EMILE: Oh. Uh...OK. What do I have to do, then?

DANE: From what you've read in the book, what do you think?
[*A pause*]

EMILE: Well, Jon and Brant always pray with people. So, I need to pray, I guess. But not the Hail Mary thing my mom does, right?

DANE: Right. It needs to be your own words. And what do you think you need to tell God?

EMILE: Um, that I want him to forgive me of all the stuff I've done. And that I believe Jesus will do that, if I believe he died and came back to life. Is that it?

DANE: Yep. Anything stopping you from doing that right now, Emile?
[*A slight pause*]

EMILE: No, I guess not. But am I gonna pray, or are you? Because, in the book, Jon does it.

DANE: I think it would be better if you do it, Emile. It's between you and God. But we'll pray silently along with you, if that's OK.

SAM: [*edges toward the front of his seat*] I'm sorry, point of protocol, if I may: Would it be best if I step out for a moment, or should I stay?

EMILE: You stay here, Sam.

SAM: Yes, of course. I just didn't know how these things work.
[*settles back in his chair*]

DANE: Anytime you're ready, Emile.

EMILE: OK, here goes.

[*The group bows their heads.*]

EMILE: [*sighs*] Hey, God. It's me, Emile. I've been reading this book and talking with the guys, here, and I think I kinda get a few things I've been missing before. I really didn't know all this stuff about being saved and born again, until I read about it. But I think I need to do that. Be born again, I mean. I don't know the right words to say, but I'm sorry that I...pushed my cousin Joey off the swing when I was five, and lied to my mom yesterday about how her hair color looked natural, and how I ate fries out of the holding bins when I worked at KFC and.... [*opens his eyes and looks to* DANE] Do I need to confess everything, or does he already know all this stuff?

[*The group lifts their heads and opens their eyes.*]

DANE: It's not a confessional, Emile. You can just admit that you've sinned and that you're sorry.

EMILE: Got it.

[*The group bows their heads and closes their eyes.*]

EMILE: OK, so anyway, God.... [*opens his eyes and looks to* DANE] Can I say I'm sorry about my dad?

[*The group lifts their heads and opens their eyes.*]

DANE: Sure, go ahead.

EMILE: OK.

[*The group bows their heads and closes their eyes.*]

EMILE: Hey God, it's me, again. I'm sorry that I've been mad at my dad all these years. I didn't want to admit that or believe I was, but I guess I have been. And maybe I've been a little mad at you, too. I never wanted to go with my mom to Mass. I just didn't see the point. I didn't think you really cared about me. But now, it's like, there's this whole new thing about you and Jesus and forgiveness and heaven and joy and stuff. And I want all that. So, I'm asking you, God, to make me a real Christian. I want Jesus to forgive me, and I believe that he died for me and came back to life and everything. I hope that's what you wanted to hear. Thanks, God...talk to you later. [*opens his eyes and lifts his head*]

DANE: [*eyes still closed*] Amen.

EMILE: [*closes his eyes*] Amen.

[*The group lifts their heads and opens their eyes.*]

EMILE: Did I do it?

DANE: Yes, you did!

EMILE: Excellent!

SAM: Congratulations, Emile.

RETT: Yes, félicitations à vous!

EMILE: Gesundheit. Hey Martin, wake-up!

[MARTIN *stirs slightly.*]

EMILE: Hey man, you missed it!

MARTIN: [*opens his eyes and lifts his head*] Missed what? Last call?

EMILE: No, dude. I just did the whole born again thing. I'm a Christian!

MARTIN: [*drops his head back on the floor*] And the rich get richer. Good for you, Emile. [*struggles to turn himself over and fails*] Can someone help me off the floor? I think rigor mortis has started to set in.

[EMILE *stands, leans down and pulls* MARTIN *up by the hand in one easy motion.*]

MARTIN: [*surprised to find himself suddenly on his feet, gestures toward* EMILE] The Incredible Hulk, ladies and gentlemen.

[SAM *begins to clap, then stops when no one else joins him.*]

[MARTIN *and* EMILE *sit down.*]

DANE: So, Emile, do you have any questions about what just happened?

EMILE: No, I don't think so. I might later, though. Oh, wait. [*closes his eyes and slaps his forehead*] What am I gonna tell my mom? She's gonna freak-out.

MARTIN: Tell her you were kidnapped by aliens, and they made you read a long book with no pictures in it.

EMILE: Dude, she might totally believe the part about aliens.

RETT: Just tell her the truth, Emile. And then give it some time. She'll be OK.

EMILE: I don't know, man. You don't know my mom.

DANE: She knows you've been coming here to church, doesn't she?

EMILE: Yeah, kind of. I haven't been completely honest with her about that.

MARTIN: Break it to her at the flea market, then buy her a nice Jesus Pez dispenser. I'm sure they have those.

DANE: Emile, I'm going to have our Pastor give you a call this week, if that's OK. Just to talk with you about next steps in your faith.

EMILE: He's not going to ask me any hard questions, is he? Like from the Bible?

DANE: No, it's not a test; I promise.

EMILE: OK. Sure, man. That would be great.

DANE: [*checks his watch*] Well, guys, it looks like it's time to wrap-up for tonight.

MARTIN: Last round on me.

DANE: Martin, your keys, please?

[MARTIN *reaches in his pocket and reluctantly tosses his keys to* DANE.]

DANE: Don't worry, you can let me out down the street like last time.

MARTIN: Thank you.

DANE: Rett, can you follow me, again?

RETT: Sure thing. Maybe we can get that cup of coffee afterwards.

DANE: I can't, tonight. I have a ton of papers to grade. Let's try again, next week.

RETT: OK. But can I make a quick suggestion?

DANE: Go ahead.

RETT: I'd like our new brother in Christ, Emile, to close us in prayer, tonight.

EMILE: Boo-yah!

DANE: I think that's a yes in any language.

EMILE: Let's pray, dudes!

[*The group bows their heads to pray and the curtain closes.*]

Curtain

ACT THREE

Scene One

DANE *enters the dark, empty classroom and flips the light switch on the wall. He places his book and notepad on the table just inside the door and, whistling cheerfully, arranges five chairs for the group. He folds the remaining chairs and leans them against the wall.* RETT *enters carrying a Starbucks coffee cup in his hand.*

DANE: Hey, Rett! [*smiles broadly as he folds a chair*] You're here early!

RETT: Evening, Dane. [*sets his book on a chair and takes a seat on the end of the row*]

[DANE *hums joyfully to himself as he puts away the last extra chair.*]

RETT: You seem unusually lively, tonight.

DANE: [*smiles*] Just excited about our group, I guess. [*sits in his chair facing the other four*] Last week was amazing, wasn't it?

RETT: [*nods*] I have to admit, I've never seen someone pass out on the floor of a men's church group, before. You're breaking new ground, Dane.

DANE: [*chuckles*] No, Emile! Wasn't that awesome?

RETT: Ah, you're still aglow about that.

DANE: Of course, I am! And you should be, too. It wouldn't have happened without you here.

RETT: [*furrows his brow*] I think I asked him one question, Dane. You did the rest.

DANE: I know, but – and I know I was a little hard on you a few weeks ago – but [*smiles*] I guess having Pastor McCasguill here with me gave me some confidence.

[RETT *frowns and looks down at his coffee.*]

DANE: I mean that. I'm glad you're here, Rett. [*A pause as* DANE *watches* RETT *stare at the cup in his hands*] Anything wrong? Something I said?

RETT: [*eyes still down*] Dane....

DANE: Yeah?

RETT: I need to be honest with you about something.

DANE: [*chuckles*] As opposed to what?

RETT: I don't mean I've been dishonest about anything, exactly. I just...haven't been totally forthcoming. And I need to confess something.

DANE: I don't know if I'm qualified to take confession from a pastor. [*chuckles*]

[*A slight pause*]

RETT: Well...about that.

DANE: About what?

RETT: About being a pastor.

DANE: Have you been offered by another church? Are you moving?

RETT: No.

DANE: Well...what, then?

[*A slight pause*]

RETT: It's something I wanted to talk with you about after our group last week. That's why I asked you to go grab some coffee.

DANE: Believe me, I would rather have been enjoying a cup of coffee than grading the book reports my kids turned in.

Either they don't understand *A Wrinkle in Time*, or their parents don't. It's hard to tell who does the homework, sometimes.

RETT: No, I understood about that. So, I tried to tell you after we dropped Martin off at his house. But you were so excited about Emile, I didn't want to be a wet blanket.

DANE: OK, so...I'm listening now. What's on your mind, Rett?

RETT: Well...I, um.... [*shakes his head and looks down*] Darn-it, Dane.

DANE: What?

RETT: The truth is... [*lifts eyes to* DANE] I got fired.

[EMILE *enters.*]

EMILE: Hey, guys. What's up? [*stops and surveys* DANE *and* RETT] Uh-oh. Who died?

DANE: Hey, Emile. No one died. We were just having sort of a private conversation.

EMILE: Oh, sorry, dude. You want me to go for a walk or something?

DANE: If you could give us just a minute.

RETT: No, Dane, I don't mind if Emile hears what I have to say. He's a brother in the faith now, and I'm comfortable sharing things with him in confidence.

EMILE: Awesome. [*moves into the room*] And don't worry, man; I'm totally cool with secret stuff.

DANE: Have a seat, Emile.

EMILE: [*takes a seat opposite* RETT] So, what's going on? Is this about Martin?

RETT: No, Emile. It's about me.

EMILE: Oh.

RETT: I know I've led everyone to believe that my journey here was of a divine nature. A new calling, as it were, in my search for—

DANE: Just tell him, Rett.

RETT: [*sighs*] The truth is, Emile, I was fired from my position as Pastor of Dead Oak Baptist Church in Brouillette.

EMILE: Dude, you got canned? What did you do?

RETT: It's not anything I did, necessarily. It was all just a big misunderstanding that started years ago. I never cleared things up, and it finally came to a head earlier this year. So, I guess you could say it's something I didn't do.

[SAM *enters.*]

SAM: Hello. [*smiles as he eyes each of the men*] Dane. Rett. Emile. [*Scattering of subdued greetings as* SAM *takes a seat next to* EMILE]

EMILE: [*to* SAM] Dude, Rett was just telling us how he got fired from his church.

SAM: Oh, my.

DANE: Emile!

EMILE: What?

DANE: Rett told you that in confidence.

EMILE: I know.

DANE: That means you don't tell other people.

EMILE: Sam's not other people. He's one of us. Right, Sam?

SAM: [*to* RETT] They let you go?

RETT: [*nods meekly*] Yes, Sam, they did.

SAM: How awful. I can't say I've ever experienced losing a job that way. One really can't get sacked from a business he owns, I don't think. But I suppose if all my clients were to take their pets elsewhere for medical attention, they would be doing the same thing, in effect. I couldn't very well call myself a veterinarian without animals to treat, now, could I? [*chuckles*]

DANE: Sam, I don't think Rett was finished telling us what happened.

SAM: Oh, forgive me. Yes, please continue.

DANE: So, Rett, what was the misunderstanding?

RETT: Well, that's another thing I need to confess. [*a pause*] I'm not really Dr. Rett McCasguill.

EMILE: Dude! Who are you, then? Like, FBI or something?

DANE: What do you mean, Rett?

RETT: I mean I don't have my doctorate. I'm just plain Rett. No Dr. McCasguill.

EMILE: I thought pretending to be a doctor was sort of against the law.

RETT: I didn't practice medicine, Emile. It's a Doctorate of Divinity. Which I don't have.

DANE: You lied about that, Rett?

RETT: I didn't lie, really. Not at first, anyway. When I got to Brouillette, I was in-between jobs and was just passing through. But I went to church there one Sunday and liked it. So, I decided to hang around a bit. I got to know some people and must have mentioned to someone that I'd attended seminary.

DANE: Did you?

RETT: Yes, I really did. I mean, I was at Southwestern for a semester the year after I got saved. I wanted to go into the ministry. But I couldn't afford it, so I didn't finish. But the more I got involved at Dead Oak, the more they wanted me to lead things. And I was fine with that. But then, one morning, I was introduced to someone as Dr. McCasguill. I didn't think much of it at the time, but I didn't correct them, either. Pretty soon after, that's what everyone called me. I was Dr. McCasguill. I met my wife there and got married. And then when the pastor retired, the church elders asked me to be the interim pastor. So, I said yes, thinking maybe this was God's way of putting me in the ministry after all. I didn't see the harm in letting them think whatever they wanted. Besides, it was just an interim position.

DANE: You were interim Pastor for six years?

RETT: No. That's the thing. After a year, they made me permanent and put my name on the church sign, out front. Dr. Ovaretton T. McCasguill, Pastor. I was stuck. It was too late to say anything. I guess after a while I started to believe it myself.

EMILE: Dude, I totally believed it. You seemed like a real pastor.

RETT: I was a real pastor, Emile. And I was good at it, too. When people really believe in you, it almost makes you become what they believe. I became Dr. McCasguill.

DANE: But why pretend with us, Rett? I mean, why lie to me like that?

[*A pause*]

RETT: I guess I didn't want to go back to being just Rett. A nobody. [*a pause*] I lost everything in Brouillette, Dane. It's a small town. My wife grew-up in that church. Her family is all there. And she was humiliated in front of everyone she knew. That's why I moved back here, alone. I had nowhere else to go.

[*A pause*]

EMILE: Dude, it's a good thing Martin's not here. He's gonna flip when he hears about this.

DANE: Emile, Martin doesn't need to know anything about this. Understand?

EMILE: Where is he, anyway?

DANE: [*shrugs*] No idea. But what Rett shared needs to stay with the people in this room.

SAM: Count on me not to say a word.

RETT: Thanks, Sam. I just hope you guys can forgive me.

EMILE: Hey, dude, don't sweat it. We all screw-up sometime or another. One time at KFC, I dumped a whole bag of frozen chicken nuggets into the fryer. Those things came shooting out like hot missiles. Grease went everywhere. I almost got fired, too, so I know how it feels.

RETT: Thank you, Emile. I feel better knowing that.

DANE: Rett, I'm just glad you leveled with us. We're not going to judge you here, OK? Just be Rett; that's good enough for us.

RETT: Thank you, Dane.

[SAM *raises his hand.*]

DANE: Yes, Sam. And you don't have to raise your hand.

SAM: Oh, sorry.

DANE: It's OK. Go ahead.

SAM: Well, I don't know if this is the appropriate time, but I have something I'd like to share, as well.

EMILE: Let me guess: You're not really a veterinarian.

SAM: No, I am a veterinarian. Why would you guess that?

EMILE: [*slowly*] Because of...the whole pretending to be a doctor thing...that we just...never mind.

DANE: What is it, Sam?

SAM: [*takes a deep breath*] Well, I gathered the nerve to call Ms. Walker last Saturday morning shortly after ten a.m., just as Martin suggested.

DANE: Did you ask her to the Fur Ball?

SAM: No, but I did ask if she would like to sit with me in church Sunday. Which I thought, you see, may lead to an opportunity to have lunch with her afterwards. Which it did. And there I could possibly ask about the Fur Ball.

RETT: Very clever, Sam.

SAM: Yes, thank you. And it all went perfectly well until, over lunch, I asked her what type of books she enjoyed reading. Since Martin had already revealed the titles she had taken on loan from the library, it seemed a rather safe question. I had put quite a bit of thought into what to ask, you see. It may surprise you to learn that casual conversation can be a bit laborsome for me, at times.

DANE: No, we haven't noticed that; have we guys?

RETT: No, not at all.

EMILE: [*surprised*] You guys really didn't notice that?

DANE: [*ignores* EMILE] Go ahead, Sam.

SAM: Well, that being the case, I came prepared for our lunch with a list of questions. [*pulls a notepad from his sport coat pocket and opens it*]

EMILE: Let me see. [*reaches toward* SAM]
    [SAM *hands his notepad to* EMILE.]

EMILE: [*reads from the notepad*] Who is your favorite canine from TV or film? [*chuckles*] Has Major Tom experienced any more gastric discomfort since your last office visit? [*looks at* SAM *and laughs*] Dude, seriously? [*shakes his head and reads again from the notepad*] What type of books do you enjoy reading? What color are your eyes? You scratched through that one. [*hands the notepad back to* SAM]

SAM: Yes, I realized I'd be looking at her when I asked it, so it seemed a rather silly question.

DANE: And you said something went wrong when you asked her about books?

SAM: Oh, yes. Well, she claimed she didn't enjoy reading at all, which struck me as rather odd, given what Martin had observed. So, I asked her how often she goes to the library. And this is where things got a bit concerning. [*leans forward*] She said she has never been to the library.

[*A slight pause as* SAM *glances around knowingly*]

DANE: Um....

SAM: Yes, my thought exactly. I asked myself, why would she lie about reading books and going to the library? The answer was all too obvious, I'm afraid.

DANE: It was?

SAM: Yes. I could only assume she lied to conceal her illicit rendezvous with Martin. [*shakes his head*] Very disappointing. I had hoped she might accompany me to the Fur Ball, but I don't quite see the point in asking, now. I can't tolerate deception.

RETT: Yeah, a lot of people feel that way.

DANE: Maybe there's a perfectly logical explanation, Sam.

EMILE: Yeah, maybe she forgot.

DANE: [*to* EMILE] I said a logical explanation.

RETT: Guys, Sam's right. If she can't be honest with him over something simple like that, maybe it's best that he not pursue a relationship with her. [*looks down*] I can't believe I just said that.

EMILE: I think we should vote on it. All in favor of Sam asking the cat woman to the dance, raise your hand. [*raises his hand and looks around*]

[DANE *raises his hand.*]

EMILE: OK, that's two for and two against. We need Martin for the tiebreaker.

DANE: All right, well, while we wait for that to happen, why don't we talk about what we read in the book this week? That is why we're here. [*opens his notebook*] Let's see...in chapter forty-three, Jon and Brant arrive in Tallahassee and run into a street preacher on the campus of FSU.

SAM: A fellow Englishman, I might add. I was rather pleased about that.

DANE: What did you guys think of Liam? Have you ever run into someone preaching in public like that?

EMILE: There used to be this guy who walked around downtown all the time in a white robe, wearing a sign that said, "Repent or burn!" He came into KFC once.

DANE: Did he say anything?

EMILE: Not really. He just ordered a three-piece snack and sat down and ate it. I guess even crazy dudes love chicken.

DANE: Do you think that kind of evangelism, if you can call it that, reaches people?

EMILE: It didn't do anything for me. And as far as the guy in the book goes, it didn't sound like anyone was paying any attention to what he was saying.

RETT: Personally, I've never attempted to preach to an audience that wasn't there to listen. So, I'm not sure how effective preaching the Gospel to random people passing by would be. At best, it's a rather clumsy way of hoping to start a conversation with someone who may stop to argue or ask questions, like the girl did in the book.

DANE: I agree. But it worked with Brooke, didn't it?

RETT: Yes, but why create a spectacle, when all you really want is a conversation?

DANE: Well, picnics bring out the ants.

EMILE: [*to* SAM] That was a metaphor.

SAM: Actually, I believe it was more of an analogy.

EMILE: [*frowns*] Oh.

DANE: OK, next question. [*reading from his notebook*] The book seems to be making a subtle case for divine providence, while at the same time arguing against the "all things are meant to be" philosophy, as Jon did in chapter forty-six. How do you reconcile those two schools of thought?

[*A pause*]

EMILE: Um, could you repeat the question? And maybe use different words?

[MARTIN *appears in the doorway.*]

MARTIN: He's asking if we're all puppets in God's grand marionette theater or simply free-range chickens.

DANE: [*happily*] Martin! Come on in.

[MARTIN *moves into the room.*]

EMILE: Dude, we didn't think you were coming.

MARTIN: [*sits next to* RETT] I made a brief appearance at the real AA meeting in the gym, tonight.

RETT: Wow, what prompted that?

MARTIN: Well, seeing as how I couldn't remember being here last week or how I got home last Wednesday night, I thought maybe I should give the purveyors of sobriety a chance.

DANE: A wise choice, Martin.

EMILE: So, like, you don't remember passing out on the floor here last week?

MARTIN: Unfortunately – or fortunately – no.

DANE: Martin, you don't remember anything you shared with us last week? [*glances at* RETT]

MARTIN: No. Why? What did I say? I didn't tell you about sleeping with Herman, did I?

SAM: Blast it, Martin! Is there any form of depravity you won't sink to? First Ms. Walker, now this Herman fellow?

MARTIN: Herman is a stuffed animal, Sam.

SAM: A what?

MARTIN: I sleep with a stuffed animal. [*to* DANE] I didn't share that embarrassing tidbit last week?

DANE: [*smiles*] No. But thanks for sharing it this week.

EMILE: [*laughs*] Dude, you still sleep with a stuffed animal?

MARTIN: Yes, I do. When you sleep next to a block of ice named Judith, you have to do something to keep warm.

DANE: Wow, there's a rabbit hole waiting to be explored. Martin, you want to talk about that?

MARTIN: Something tells me I may already have.

EMILE: [*to* DANE] Hey, Martin can vote for Sam now that he's here!

MARTIN: What are we voting for? Chief Dogcatcher?

EMILE: No, we took a vote on whether Sam should ask out the cat woman since she lied to him.

MARTIN: [*to* SAM] Hannah lied to you? That implies that you had an actual conversation with her.

SAM: Yes, I did. I phoned her, just as you suggested last week.

MARTIN: I did?

[SAM *nods in affirmation.*]

MARTIN: I did.

SAM: Yes, you said to call her between ten and ten-thirty in the morning.

MARTIN: [*chuckles*] Why would I say that?

SAM: You said that's when she'd be most receptive to social invitations.

[MARTIN *laughs.*]

SAM: And you were quite right.

MARTIN: Wow. I must be smarter than I thought. What other sage advice did I give you?

SAM: You encouraged me to invite her to the Fur Ball, as my date.

MARTIN: The Fur Ball? What on earth is that?

SAM: We discussed this last week, Martin. It's a formal affair to raise funds for homeless pets.

DANE: Martin, Sam had lunch with Hannah after church Sunday, and she denied ever having been to the library.

MARTIN: Oh…I see.

SAM: Yes, and she also denied any interest in reading books. She was obviously lying to hide her interest in you, Martin. I don't know how, but you've corrupted that poor girl, completely. You should be ashamed of yourself.

MARTIN: Well, I am ashamed of myself but not for that reason.

SAM: And why not?

MARTIN: Because she wasn't lying.

SAM: What do you mean?

MARTIN: Sam, I've never even met your precious Ms. Walker.

RETT: What?

EMILE: Huh?

SAM: But she came into your library.

MARTIN: Nope.

SAM: You said she checked out books.

MARTIN: Totally made up.

SAM: And that she met you for drinks.

MARTIN: Never happened.

SAM: And that she likes me.

MARTIN: Now, that is the truth. She does like you, Sam. It's obvious to everyone but you. That's all I was trying to help you to see.

SAM: But you lied.

MARTIN: Sure, I did. But it was for your own good.

SAM: That hardly makes it right.

MARTIN: Would you have called Hannah if I hadn't told you all that?

SAM: More than likely not.

MARTIN: See? You should be thanking me.

SAM: But how did you even know her name?

MARTIN: You told me. Think about it. [*A pause as* MARTIN *waits for* SAM *to respond*] OK, bad idea. Don't think about it. Just believe me; I never said her name until you did.

SAM: Well, so…. [*pauses*] If you never met her…then she was telling the truth.

MARTIN: [*nods*] Keep going.

SAM: And that would mean…I have no reason to be put out with her.

MARTIN: And…?

[*A pause. Everyone looks at* SAM.]

EMILE: OK, time for a re-vote. Who's in favor of Sam asking Hannah to the Hair Ball?

DANE: Fur Ball.

EMILE: To the Fur Ball. Raise your hand.

[EMILE, DANE, RETT *and* MARTIN *raise their hands and look at* SAM.]

DANE: How 'bout it Sam?

[SAM *slowly raises his hand with a cautious smile.*]

MARTIN: [*sighs*] Finally.

EMILE: Excellent! Dude, this is gonna be just like Jon and Amy from the book.

DANE: [*chuckles*] How's that, Emile?

EMILE: You know, two people that like each other but take forever to get together.

DANE: So, you think Jon and Amy will end up together in the end?

EMILE: Dude, they better.

MARTIN: I wouldn't be so sure about that.

DANE: Why not, Martin?

MARTIN: Well, since you've read the book, you obviously know how it ends. But, so far, it reads more like a tragedy than a comedy, in the classical definition. So, I don't expect a happy ending.

DANE: That all depends how you define a happy ending.

MARTIN: Unless there's a new definition of the word "happy," I don't think it does.

RETT: Martin, I think this goes back to the discussion we were having when you walked in over how we interpret life's events. Do you think everything that happens is meant to be or not?

MARTIN: I sincerely hope not.

RETT: OK, why do you say that? [*glances at* DANE]

MARTIN: I have my reasons.

DANE: We're here to listen, Martin, if you'd like to tell us.

MARTIN: Let's just say, I would rather believe that life is a series of random, uncontrollable events of which we are either spectators or participants. Nothing more.

RETT: So, no accountability? No blame or guilt?

MARTIN: Exactly.

EMILE: [*to* MARTIN] Dude, you should meet my mom. She's the exact opposite. To her, everything is a sign from God. A couple years ago, she saw Jesus' face in a burrito. She still has it. It's in our freezer.

DANE: Well, hopefully, we can land somewhere between those two extremes. Sam, what do you think?

SAM: To be honest, I'm never really comfortable thinking about such things. There's no way to be certain of the answer, so pondering the question seems rather pointless. My aunt Gretchen used to go on quite a bit about the Almighty and life's purpose. She spent most of her time involved in various religious activities, going to services and meetings. But as I recall, she never seemed at peace with any of it.

DANE: Aunt Gretchen wouldn't have been married to your uncle with the drinking problem, would she?

SAM: Uncle Benedict. Yes, as a matter of fact, she was. My mother always mused over whether my aunt's religion drove my uncle to drink, or his drinking drove my aunt to religion. Either way, they both seemed rather lost in the end.

DANE: OK, so let me ask you, Sam, how does your perception of religion fit with what you've been reading in our book?

SAM: Well, it doesn't, really. From what I've discerned thus far, and I hope I'm correct in saying this, the central theme of the book seems to be belief rather than religion. I've never thought of the two in separate terms before, but I believe that's the case.

RETT: Dane, if I could interject here.

DANE: Sure, Rett.

RETT: Sam, in keeping with that theme, I'm curious to know what you believe.

SAM: [*shifts in his chair*] What do I believe?

RETT: Yes. [*winks at* DANE]

SAM: What do I believe...?

RETT: Mmhmm.

[*A slight pause*]

SAM: I suppose I would have to give that proper thought before answering.

RETT: Take your time.

[*A pause as* SAM *mulls it over*]

MARTIN: [*to* DANE] How long do we have this room for?

DANE: Sam, why don't you think about it over the next week, and we can discuss it next time we get together?

SAM: All right. I'll make a point to do just that.

MARTIN: And make sure you think about it between seven-thirty and nine in the evening. That's when veterinarians are more inclined to reach religious conclusions. [*grins*]

[SAM *reaches into his coat pocket and pulls out his notepad.*]

DANE: Sam. [*shakes his head*]

[MARTIN *chuckles.*]

SAM: Ah. Kidding, again?

DANE: Yes.

SAM: [*returns his notepad to his pocket*] I can never be sure with Martin. He was quite right about phoning Hannah, after all.

MARTIN: So, it's Hannah, now. No more Ms. Walker?

SAM: Well, if I'm going to ask her to the Fur Ball, I suppose I should be more familiar.

MARTIN: There's hope for you yet, Sam.

SAM: I certainly hope so.

DANE: Guys, unless anyone has anything else, why don't we stop there for tonight?

EMILE: [*raises his hand slightly*] I have something.

DANE: Sure, Emile.

EMILE: I'm getting baptized this Sunday. And I'd like all you guys to be there.

DANE: That's great, man!

EMILE: Yeah. And I talked to my mom. She's going to come with me to church Sunday, so she'll be here to see me get dunked.

RETT: That's huge, Emile.

EMILE: Yeah, so you were right, Rett. I just leveled with her. She was upset at first, that I wasn't coming back to her church, but after a few days, she was OK with it.

MARTIN: I feel like I missed something.

DANE: Emile made a decision to accept Christ last week.

EMILE: Yeah, dude, while you were asleep on the floor, right there. [*motions toward the floor*]

MARTIN: Can we just pretend last week didn't happen?

EMILE: As far as you're concerned, it didn't.

[DANE *and* RETT *laugh.*]

MARTIN: That's a fair point.

DANE: Martin, last week is history. We're just glad you came back and that you're trying to get some help.

MARTIN: Thank you. And I assume you drove me home last week.

DANE: Yes. You slept all the way. Did you make it into your house, OK? It looked like you were having trouble with your key when we left.

MARTIN: Actually, I woke-up in the bushes next to our front door sometime during the night.

RETT: [*to* DANE] You were right. We should've helped him inside.

DANE: Sorry about that, Martin. We'll know next time.

MARTIN: If I want to stay married, there can't be a next time.

DANE: Well, just remember, Martin, we're here to help.

[*A slight pause*]

MARTIN: I actually believe that.

DANE: [*smiles*] I'll count that as progress. Rett, would you mind praying for us, and we'll get out of here?

RETT: I'd be honored.

[*The group bows their heads to pray and the curtain closes.*]

Curtain

ACT THREE

Scene Two

DANE *and* RETT *enter the dark, empty classroom both carrying cups of coffee from the Lost Bean.* DANE *flips the light switch on the wall.*

DANE: Just admit it, Rett!

RETT: Different is not synonymous with better, Dane.

DANE: I saw the look on your face when you sipped it. I know you think it's good. [*sets his notepad and book down on the table against the wall*]

RETT: I was simply thinking of the French toast I had for breakfast this morning. It was très bon.

DANE: [*rolls his eyes*] Whatever.

RETT: I like Starbucks, Dane. Why can't you accept that?

DANE: So, you're going to stand there and tell me that burnt, overly roasted, cheap Robusta coffee beans make better tasting coffee than Arabica? [*points to the cup in* RETT's *hand*]

RETT: What's Arabica?

DANE: [*throws his hands up*] Oh my gosh! Never mind. [*begins arranging the five chairs for the group*]

RETT: [*watches* DANE] Dane, if you ever get this passionate about sharing the Gospel, you'll be the next Billy Graham.

DANE: Yeah, yeah. Help me put these chairs away.

143

[DANE *and* RETT *begin folding the extra chairs and leaning them against the wall.*]

RETT: Incidentally, I finally finished your manuscript last night.

DANE: [*pauses*] You did? What did you think?

RETT: [*folds a chair and moves it to the wall*] I really liked it. I couldn't help but think of you as the main character, though. Did all that stuff really happen?

DANE: No, of course not. [*begins folding chairs, again*] It's fiction. And I'm definitely not Delancey Tate.

RETT: Well, you said it was autobiographical. [*sits down in a chair at the end of the row, crosses his legs and sips his coffee*]

DANE: [*continues putting chairs away*] Only in the sense that I used my own experiences to come up with fictional story lines for the characters. All writers do that. [*leans the last extra chair against the wall*]

RETT: Still, an uptight, divorced English lit professor, who obsesses over coffee, sounds a lot like someone else I know.

DANE: [*grabs his notebook and book from the table and takes a seat in his group leader chair*] Well, most readers won't have your inside knowledge, Rett. I'm curious to know what you thought of the ending.

RETT: I actually had a question about that. Was the killer really the grad assistant? Because it seemed like you left some doubt there. I had the dean pegged the whole time.

DANE: I left that intentionally vague in case I needed to write a sequel. That's what publishers want these days. One book's not enough.

[SAM *enters.*]

DANE: Hey, Sam.

SAM: Hello, Dane, Rett.

RETT: Ça va, Sam?

SAM: Sorry?

DANE: Rett, can we not start with the French thing, again?

[SAM *takes a seat next to* RETT.]

RETT: It's a common greeting, Dane.

DANE: In France.

SAM: Ah, you asked how I am in French. I do speak the language, but my ears weren't prepared for it. I'm more accustomed to translating American English to my native equivalent than I am listening for French. But I'm well, thank you. Or "Bien!" as they say across the Channel.

DANE: We're not across the Channel or in Louisiana. So, let's just stick to English, OK, guys?

RETT: [*to* SAM] Dane est un peu nerveux, n'est-il pas?

SAM: [*laughs*] Yes, I believe he is.

DANE: All right, very funny. Have your little joke. That's fine.

[MARTIN *enters*.]

MARTIN: Bonjour!

DANE: Oh, come on!

MARTIN: [*stops*] What?

DANE: [*points at* RETT] Did he tell you to say that?

MARTIN: Did he tell me to say hello?

DANE: Yes, in French.

MARTIN: [*sits next to* SAM] No, but he did tell me to say you seem a little uptight this evening.

[RETT *looks at* DANE *and shakes his head in denial*.]

SAM: [*to* MARTIN] He just said the same to me in French.

DANE: [*to* RETT] That's what you said?

RETT: Well, you do seem a little on edge tonight, Dane. [*grins*] Maybe that coffee of yours has extra caffeine to make up for its lack of flavor.

DANE: Lack of– [*stops, closes his eyes, takes a deep breath and exhales*] OK. I'm just going to hit the reset button and move on.

RETT: I'm sorry. It was just a little humor.

DANE: I know, Rett. I've just had a long day, that's all.

MARTIN: Too many homework assignments eaten by dogs?

DANE: No. That I could handle.

RETT: So, what's bothering you, Dane?

[*A slight pause*]

DANE: [*sighs*] I guess I might as well share my news. [*pauses*] I heard from my agent today.

RETT: About your book?

DANE: Yeah.

MARTIN: [*grins*] So, what's the word, Dave?

DANE: She did call me "Dane" this time, thank you, Martin. But it seems the publisher she's been talking with decided to pass on my book.

RETT: Dane, I'm sorry.

DANE: Yeah, well....

RETT: I happen to think your book is intriguing and very well written.

DANE: Funny thing is, Rett, they actually agreed with you.

RETT: I don't understand; then why'd they pass?

DANE: They said it was too long for its market price range. Production costs would eat into their margins.

RETT: And that means what, exactly?

DANE: It means they want me to edit ten thousand words out, just so they can earn a few more cents on the dollar. I told my agent I wouldn't do it. So, she dropped me as a client. End of story. End of book. [*drops his gaze to the notebook on his lap and shakes his head*] Whatever. It was all just a waste of time, anyway.

[*A pause*]

[MARTIN, SAM *and* RETT *exchange glances.*]

MARTIN: Dane, if you have an extra copy of your manuscript, I wouldn't mind reading it.

[DANE *looks up at* MARTIN.]

RETT: It's very good, Martin. You'd like it.

SAM: I'd enjoy having a copy, too, Dane, if it's no trouble.

MARTIN: [*looks to* RETT *and* SAM] And maybe we could meet here to discuss it on Wednesday nights. Like we're doing now. Otherwise, I'll be stuck going to the AA meeting.

RETT: Count me in. Sam, how about you?

SAM: Yes, of course. We're almost through this book, and it would be nice to continue meeting. I've grown rather fond of our Wednesday night discussions.

DANE: [*smiles*] You guys would really want to do that?

RETT: Absolutely.

SAM: And hopefully Emile could join us, as well.

RETT: [*to* DANE] Where is he tonight, anyway?

DANE: I don't know. [*pulls his phone from his pocket*] He sent me a text this morning. [*reads from his phone*] It just said, "Dude. Out of town on business. Haha. See you next week."

RETT: On business?

MARTIN: Haha.

RETT: What kind of business?

DANE: I don't know. That's all he said.

MARTIN: There must be a comic book convention somewhere.

DANE: I guess we'll find out next week. Do you guys want to go ahead and dig into our book?

RETT: Sure.

[SAM *and* MARTIN *nod.*]

DANE: OK, let's see. [*opens his notebook and flips a few pages*] Here we go. These four chapters had our guys heading home for Christmas and then back out to Texas. Any initial thoughts from what you read for this week?

SAM: I enjoyed the chapter where the boy played with the Anatolian shepherd on Christmas Eve. Very clever breed, the Anatolians. A bit too smart for their own good, at times.

MARTIN: "Cleverness is not wisdom."

DANE: Euripides?

MARTIN: For an English lit teacher, you know your Greek tragedies.

DANE: I only teach English lit; I read everything.

RETT: Martin, you're full of these quotes, but I wonder if you ever think about what they mean.

MARTIN: Ah, a challenge from the ex-pastor. Do go on, sir.

RETT: All right, I would say you're a pretty clever guy.

MARTIN: Agreed. [*chuckles*]

RETT: But would you say you're wise?

MARTIN: [*ponders the question for a moment*] "The only true wisdom is in knowing you know nothing." So according to that definition from Socrates, I'm the wisest one here. Actually, Sam may win the prize on that basis.

SAM: Thank you, Martin.

MARTIN: [*chuckles*] You're welcome. You, on the other hand, dear Pastor, pretend to know everything and call it wisdom. I call it being delusional.

RETT: I don't pretend to know everything, Martin. But I'm certain that God does, and that's where my wisdom comes from.

MARTIN: [*laughs*] The wisest man in the Bible said, "Everything is meaningless." Proof that your definition of wisdom only leads to a miserable dead end. I'd rather be a clever fool than a miserable ex-pastor.

RETT: Well, I'd rather be a miserable ex-pastor than a—

DANE: Whoa, guys. Let's dial it back a bit. This isn't a cage match. We're just talking.

MARTIN: No, let him finish. You'd rather be an ex-pastor than a what?

[RETT *remains silent.*]

MARTIN: Go ahead and say it.

RETT: Martin—

MARTIN: A drunk? A failure? Isn't that what you were going to say?

RETT: Maybe.

MARTIN: Oh…well, all right, then.

RETT: Martin, there's something you should know.

MARTIN: You have a few more degrading words of wisdom for me? Oh, joy. Please preach on, Pastor.

RETT: No, I owe you an apology.

MARTIN: No, you don't. You see, that's the difference between you and me. At least I know what I am. I can look in the mirror every day and see exactly what the world sees: A crummy little assistant librarian in a crummy little library. I don't carry divine delusions of grandeur around to impress people.

RETT: You're not making this any easier.

MARTIN: Tell me, what do you see when you look in the mirror, Dr. McCasguill?

[*A slight pause*]

RETT: Martin, you weren't here last week when I shared this, but I'm not a doctor.

MARTIN: But you play one on TV, is that it?

RETT: No. Seriously, I never earned that title. I've been less than honest about that for years, and I was fired by my church over it. I've shamed myself and my family. I moved back here alone because I had nowhere else to go. So, you ask who I see when I look in the mirror? I see someone I don't know.

[*A pause*]

MARTIN: I, uh....

RETT: The real difference between you and me, Martin, is that I know where to go to find redemption. Through God's grace, I have forgiveness. But I'm hoping you can forgive me, too.

MARTIN: Me? You don't need my forgiveness.

RETT: No, I suppose I don't. But I would like to have it, if you'd be gracious enough to offer it.

[*A slight pause*]

MARTIN: All right, fine. I hereby pardon you of all false, deceptive, overbearing, condescending and otherwise pedantic representations of yourself to me and to the group. How's that?

RETT: I guess I asked for that.

MARTIN: [*smiles*] Yes, you did.

RETT: I'll take it. Thank you, Martin.

MARTIN: You're welcome, Rett.

[*A slight pause*]

DANE: Well, that was interesting. Thank you, guys. Um...Sam, I believe you were talking about the Christmas chapter.

SAM: Yes, I believe I was.

DANE: Did you have anything more to add about that, or were you finished?

SAM: Well, it did remind me of one particular Christmas from my youth. My uncle Winston and aunt Phoebe had come over from Royal Tunbridge Wells to spend Christmas Eve with us and help trim the tree. They're quite well off, you know. Phoebe is my mother's sister and married Winston on a lark after a romantic encounter in Hastings one summer. My mother always said, "Marriage is a gamble, but Phoebe won the scratchcard of life when she married Winston." He'd made a fortune selling socks to the military. So, my mother took their visit on Christmas Eve as quite the honor. But I doubt they would have come had they known Aunt Gretchen and Uncle Benedict would be there. Not a good match, those four. Made for quite an evening. Winston and Benedict got into a row over support stockings, and Gretchen and Phoebe would only speak to my mother but not to each other. They ended up having their tea in separate rooms with my mother running back and forth. Later, I found Uncle Benedict lying barefoot, asleep under the tree.

[MARTIN *laughs.*]

DANE: How old were you, Sam?

SAM: Eleven. I remember because it was the same Christmas I got Pim.

RETT: Pim?

SAM: Yes. A purebred English foxhound. [*smiles warmly*] We were inseparable, Pim and I. He's actually the reason I became a veterinarian. Although, I suppose I should give Uncle Benedict credit for that. He gave Pim to me that very night. Best Christmas of my life.

DANE: Where was your father in all this?

SAM: We lost Dad when I was just two.

DANE: Oh, I'm sorry.

RETT: How, Sam?

SAM: Hunting accident, I'm afraid.

RETT: Oh, gosh.

DANE: That's horrible.

SAM: Yes. He and Uncle Benedict – they were brothers, you see – were hunting pheasant in Selsfield Common. It seems Uncle Benedict intended to flush the birds from some tall grass by throwing a stone towards them. He was quite the bowler in the Sussex cricket league back then. Very strong arm, you know. He once dismissed all eleven batsmen in a match. Or so they say. It's always been rather hard to fathom, knowing him later in life, as I did.

MARTIN: So, what happened?

SAM: Ah, well, while Uncle Benedict was foraging about for a stone to hurl at the birds, Dad had bent over to tie his bootlace. When Benedict found a stone about the size of a cricket ball, he wound up and let it go just as my father stood straight. The stone struck him in the head and knocked him clean out.

DANE: [*shakes his head*] I'm sure your uncle felt horrible.

SAM: Yes, quite. When Dad came to few minutes later, he had a few choice words for his brother, as you could imagine.

RETT: OK, so…I'm confused. How did your father pass away, then, Sam?

SAM: Oh, he died two days later, sitting at the breakfast table with my mother eating a bowl of Coco Shreddies. The knock to his head caused an epidural hemorrhage, you see. Blood on the brain. Very sad.

RETT: I'm sorry for your loss, Sam.

MARTIN: What are Coco Shreddies?

DANE: [*ignores* MARTIN] So, Sam, I'm guessing this is why your uncle drank the way he did? Guilt over your father's death, maybe? [*glances at* MARTIN]

SAM: Oh. Well, I don't know. I've never considered that possibility, really. He was always that way as long as I knew him. Just saucy old Uncle Benedict.

MARTIN: Are you trying to imply something, Dane? I couldn't help but notice your glance my way a second ago.

DANE: No, not at all. I was just—

MARTIN: Maybe old Uncle Benedict just enjoyed a pint or two every now and then. What's wrong with that? Maybe guilt had nothing to do with it. Why does everyone have to psychoanalyze someone for enjoying a few drinks?

RETT: "Me thinks thou dost protest too much."

MARTIN: Nice try, Doc, but that's not even the quote.

RETT: I believe it is. It's from *Macbeth*.

MARTIN: No, it's from *Hamlet*, and it's, "The lady doth protest too much, methinks."

RETT: Well, that wouldn't work for obvious reasons. But my point was that your defense of Uncle Benedict seems a bit personal, Martin.

MARTIN: Of course it's personal. Everything I say is personal, because I'm the person saying it.

RETT: [*sighs and looks to* DANE] A little help, here?

DANE: Martin, I was simply posing the question about the possible reason for Uncle Benedict's drinking. It's a perfectly logical assumption that Sam's father's death may have been a burden that led him to seek comfort in alcohol.

MARTIN: If you're going to turn this into a real AA group, I might as well go down the hall to the gym. At least they have coffee and doughnuts there.

DANE: All right, never mind. I'll change the subject. For now.

MARTIN: Why don't you ask Sam about his homework assignment? I'm dying to know the answer.

DANE: What homework assignment?

RETT: I think we asked Sam to give some thought to his beliefs over the last week.

DANE: Oh, gosh. I totally forgot.

MARTIN: I was actually referring to his assignment to call the lovely Ms. Hannah. Any news for us, Sam?

SAM: Um, well–

RETT: Let's come back to that one, if that's OK, Sam.

SAM: Certainly.

RETT: Did you have time to mull things over since last week? About your beliefs?

SAM: Well, I found your question to be strangely coincidental to the first chapter we read for this week.

DANE: The airplane discussion?

SAM: Yes. Our man Jon posed basically the same question to his acquaintance on the plane. And as I read, I began to feel more and more as if I were part of the conversation.

DANE: How so, Sam?

SAM: Well, I found I had a few things in common with the businessman to whom Jon spoke. I also run a company of sorts, albeit a much smaller one. I have ten on staff, not including volunteers. Not that volunteers are any less important, mind you. They do perform some of the more thankless tasks and always seem cheerful going about them. Although, at times, they can be a rather curious lot. For instance, I tried to offer a small compensation to one of them last summer, just out of gratitude, and she became rather indignant with me. She said, "If you think I'm going to clean up after all these animals for that, you're crazy." When I pointed out that she'd been happily doing the same task for free prior to my offer, she quit and stomped out of my office. I'm still not certain if I offered too much or too little. [*shakes his head in thought*]

[MARTIN *chuckles to himself.*]

DANE: Sam, I think you've gotten a little sidetracked from Rett's question.

SAM: Oh, yes. Where was I?

DANE: To be honest, I'm not sure.

SAM: Hmm. Ah! I remember. Yes. I was about to say that, as a business owner, I take great care to accommodate the beliefs and interests of my employees, not unlike the gentleman on the plane.

DANE: Geoff Holland.

SAM: Yes, thank you. Just as Mr. Holland did at his company.

MARTIN: His fictional company.

DANE: Martin, I think we all understand that this is a work of fiction. No one is saying otherwise.

MARTIN: Just keeping it real.

DANE: Please go ahead, Sam.

SAM: Right. Well, as I read how Mr. Holland was quizzed about his beliefs, I began to share in his discomfort over his inability to provide sound answers.

RETT: You're saying you aren't sure what you believe, Sam?

SAM: Yes. At least I was uncertain. Now, I may not be.

MARTIN: You're not certain if you're uncertain or not? [*chuckles*]

DANE: Martin.

MARTIN: [*shrugs*] Sorry.

RETT: Tell us what you mean, Sam.

SAM: Well, I suppose it was the quote Jon offered from C.S. Lewis. The question of who Jesus was.

RETT: Was he a lunatic, liar or the Son of God?

SAM: Yes.

MARTIN: That question presupposes that Jesus was a real person.

DANE: Of course, it does.

MARTIN: But you're pretending to make a logical argument based on a false premise.

DANE: You're saying Jesus wasn't a real person?

MARTIN: Well, how do you know he was? How do you know it wasn't all just made up?

RETT: Martin, you would have to explain away over two thousand years of human history to believe that the man Jesus didn't exist. Are you prepared to do that?

MARTIN: Well, no…not at the moment.

RETT: All right, then. Let's let Sam have his say.

MARTIN: Fine.

RETT: Sam, in your own mind, how do you answer that question?

SAM: And which question are we on, then?

RETT: The question of who Jesus was. Was he a liar, a crazy person, or was he really who he claimed to be: the Son of God?

[MARTIN *sighs and rolls his eyes.*]

SAM: Yes, of course. I must say, that particular question led me to a fair amount of reading and thinking over the last week.

MARTIN: Poor, lad. You must be exhausted.

RETT: [*ignores* MARTIN] And what did you conclude, Sam?

SAM: Well, based on what I understand, I would have to say his motives were too pure and selfless to be considered dishonest, which makes him being a liar rather unlikely. And from what I read, I see no indication of mental instability, unless of course you consider his rejection of societal norms of the day insanity, which would also have to apply to any number of perfectly sane but free-thinking individuals across history. So, I tend to rule that out as well.

RETT: You know that only leaves one option, Sam.

SAM: Yes, I know.

RETT: So, if you believe that Jesus is the Son of God, you have no choice but to see your life on his terms.

SAM: And what terms are those?

RETT: You have to acknowledge that he is the only path to knowing God. He's the only way you can have a relationship with God.

MARTIN: Sam, you don't have to go along with this, you know. You can–

SAM: Martin, I say this with all due respect, but please do shut up for a moment.

[RETT *and* DANE *smile in surprise.*]

MARTIN: Shut up?

SAM: Yes. If you don't mind.

MARTIN: [*to* DANE *and* RETT] You see that? [*points to* SAM] Standing up for himself, now. I think I've been a good influence on him.

DANE: Seriously?

RETT: Sam let's don't lose the moment here. You have basic belief, but you need to take the next step.

SAM: And what step is that, exactly?

RETT: You've read enough in this book to understand what it means to become a Christian. You've seen the Gospel explained several times. You have to admit that you're a sinner and ask God to forgive you, knowing that Jesus paid the price for your sins on the Cross. You need to accept him as your Lord and Savior.

SAM: Oh, that. I did that Saturday.

RETT: You what?

SAM: Yes. I made a decision to believe what I had been reading and prayed a prayer to God, just as you described. I must say, the book was most helpful as far as examples go.

DANE: So…I'm sorry, I'm trying to absorb this. You're a Believer, Sam?

SAM: Yes, I suppose I am.

RETT: [*laughing*] That's great, Sam!

DANE: Congratulations, Sam!

SAM: Thank you.

MARTIN: Have you told Hannah?

SAM: As a matter of fact, I have.

MARTIN: You called her?

SAM: I did. And she was most excited to hear it. In fact, she let loose a rather high-pitched squeal into the phone that left my ear ringing. [*rubs his ear*]

MARTIN: And did you ask her out?

SAM: No, I'm afraid not.

MARTIN: [*huffs*] Honestly, Sam. Why didn't you?

SAM: I fully intended to, Martin, but she asked me first. [*smiles*] I'm escorting her to the Fur Ball next weekend.

MARTIN: Well, halleluiah! [*leans over and shakes* SAM's *hand*] My work here is done.

DANE: Sam, you're on a roll, tonight.

RETT: Yes, he is.

SAM: [*smiles*] Well, I'm very grateful to this group. You've made quite a difference in my thinking. And that includes you, Martin.

MARTIN: [*pretends to wipe a tear from the corner of his eye*] Our little Sam is all grown up. [*sniffs*] What ever shall we do, now?

DANE: How about we pray and call it a night. Nothing like ending on a high note. Rett, could you close us?

RETT: Sure.

SAM: Um.... [*raises his hand*]

DANE: Yes, Sam?

SAM: Would it be all right if I had a go at it, this time?

DANE: [*smiles*] By all means.

[*The group bows their heads to pray as the curtain closes.*]

Curtain

ACT THREE

Scene Three

EMILE *enters the dark, empty classroom carrying a book bag on his shoulder. He flips the light switch on the wall, revealing a smile on his face. He sets his bag down on the floor and begins moving chairs around but without an apparent design or pattern in mind.* DANE *enters.*

DANE: Hey, Emile.

EMILE: [*turns to see* DANE] Dane! [*moves toward* DANE *with his arms outstretched*] Bring it in, dude!

[DANE, *with his arms hanging at his side, receives a bear hug from* EMILE.]

DANE: Uh, OK. Good to see you, too, buddy.

EMILE: [*pats* DANE *on his back and releases him*] How's it going, man?

DANE: Good. Everything's good. [*sets his notepad and book down on a chair*] We missed you last week.

EMILE: I know. It sucked not being here. But you're gonna love the reason I missed it.

DANE: Oh, yeah?

EMILE: [*smiles*] Yeah, dude.

DANE: [*begins folding chairs and moving them to the wall*] You had some kind of business out of town? Something with your dad's estate?

EMILE: Nah, that's all settled. I'll tell you about it, but you're gonna have to wait until the other guys get here. Maybe I'll spring it on everyone at the end of class.

161

DANE: You seem awfully excited about it, whatever it is.

EMILE: That's because it's a total God thing. [*begins arranging a loose formation of chairs for the group*] You see, I talked to my mom's priest, and–

DANE: This isn't another sign, like your mother's burrito, is it?

EMILE: No, man. Nothing weird like that. Trust me, you're gonna love it.

DANE: I believe you. Have you talked with Sam since last week?

EMILE: No, why?

DANE: He's got some news, too.

EMILE: What is it?

DANE: He accepted Christ.

EMILE: No way! [*extends his arms to give* DANE *another hug*]

DANE: [*quickly folds a chair in front of him and avoids* EMILE's *hug*] Yep. He did it on his own, Saturday a week ago. And here's the kicker: He's going with Hannah to the Fur Ball, this weekend.

EMILE: Whoa! [*sits down*] Does Martin know?

DANE: Yep, he was here last week.

EMILE: Was he...you know.... [*sticks his tongue out, closes his eyes and tilts his head*]

DANE: No, he was sober, again; believe it or not. That's two weeks in a row.

EMILE: Dude, maybe he's cured. Like, God did a miracle or something.

DANE: [*begins to reform the half-hazard arrangement of chairs around* EMILE *into a smooth arc*] I doubt that's the case, Emile. Martin's masking some serious pain from losing his daughter, and I think he's got some serious guilt to go along with it. [*sits down in his group leader chair*] I'm going to try and see if I can get him talking about some of that tonight.

EMILE: I like Martin. Even if he is kind of….

DANE: Difficult sometimes?

EMILE: I was gonna say jerky, but that works, too. He just needs something good to happen, that's all.

[RETT *enters.*]

RETT: Dane. Emile.

EMILE: Rett! [*stands and embraces a surprised, uncomfortable* RETT] Happy to see you, dude!

RETT: I can see that. [*glances at* DANE *as he pats* EMILE *lightly on the back*]

DANE: I should have warned you, Rett. He's in a huggy mood, tonight.

[EMILE *releases* RETT.]

RETT: No, that's perfectly all right. [*straightens his shirt*] Emile, where were you last week?

EMILE: [*returns to his chair*] I was on a mission from God, man.

RETT: [*chuckles as he sits down and looks at* DANE] A mission from God, hmm? How enigmatic.

EMILE: Uh, is that French for something?

DANE: That was actually English this time, Emile. It means mysterious.

EMILE: Oh. It sounds sorta like what Sam did to Major Tom.

DANE: [*chuckles*] No, enema's not a French word, either. Although, it should be.

RETT: [*chuckles*] So, Emile, what exactly did you do on your mission from God?

DANE: He wants to keep it a secret until the end of the group, tonight.

RETT: Ah, well, I'll look forward to hearing all about it.

EMILE: You're gonna love it, dude. I promise.

[MARTIN *enters, followed closely by* SAM.]

EMILE: Hey, guys! [*stands*]

[MARTIN *ducks under* EMILE's *out-stretched arms, avoiding a hug.*]

EMILE: [*turns his attention to* SAM] Sam! [*steps forward and embraces a bewildered* SAM]

SAM: [*sounding squeezed*] Hello, Emile.

[MARTIN *takes a seat next to* RETT.]

MARTIN: [*to* RETT] Has he been drinking?

RETT: No. Just happy, I think.

EMILE: [*releases* SAM] Hey, I heard we're brothers now, dude!

SAM: Uh…. [*looks to* DANE]

DANE: He's referring to your new faith, Sam. You're now brothers in the faith.

SAM: [*sits next to* MARTIN] Ah, yes, of course. Brothers. I never had one growing up. Unless, of course, you count Pim.

MARTIN: Pim.

SAM: Yes.

MARTIN: Pim, your dog, Pim. That Pim?

SAM: Yes. He was like a brother in many ways. I learned a lot from him.

MARTIN: [*rubs his chin*] Hmm. This may explain your amiable canine-like social skills.

SAM: [*smiles*] I suppose it may, yes.

DANE: [*chuckles*] I don't think he was paying you a compliment, Sam.

SAM: Ah, but dogs are very social animals, you know. Once, when I still a boy in grammar school, we were visiting my uncle Benedict's cottage in Turner's Hill, when–

DANE: Not to cut you off Sam, but–

MARTIN: But you did cut him off. [*grins*]

DANE: I know I did, but–

MARTIN: But you can't say, "not to cut you off" and then proceed to interrupt him like you're still being polite about it.

DANE: All right. I–

MARTIN: What if I did that to you?

DANE: What, cut me off?

MARTIN: Yes. How would you like it?

DANE: Well, seeing as how you've cut me off three times in the last ten seconds, I can say, with a fair amount of confidence, that I wouldn't like it.

[*A slight pause*]

MARTIN: Oh. Well, I guess I've made my point, then. [*smiles*] Go on.

DANE: [*sighs*] Sam, I'm sorry I interrupted your story. What were you saying?

SAM: Oh, uh…I can't say I remember, now. But I think it was going to be a rather funny story, at that, whatever it was.

MARTIN: [*grins*] Well, we'll just pretend we all had a good laugh. [*chuckles*]

DANE: [*cuts his eyes at* MARTIN] OK, let me try again. I was about to ask if everyone finished the book.

EMILE: Yeah, dude, what's up with the ending?

DANE: I take that to mean you didn't like it.

EMILE: No, I didn't. I wanted to hurl my book across my bathroom.

MARTIN: Remind me to never borrow books from you.

DANE: [*chuckles*] Emile, I warned you about the ending when we started.

EMILE: Yeah, but what about Jon and Amy? I mean, come on!

DANE: Did anyone else have a similar reaction?

MARTIN: I was actually pleasantly surprised.

DANE: Wow. How so, Martin?

MARTIN: Because, if it had ended the way Emile apparently wanted it to, I would have dismissed the whole book as predictable feel-good drivel. If you want that, don't waste your time reading; just watch the Hallmark Channel.

DANE: I assume you prefer a darker edge to your stories.

MARTIN: I prefer stories that acknowledge life doesn't always have a happy ending.

RETT: I would disagree, Martin.

MARTIN: Oh, goody. I was hoping you would.

RETT: I happen to think this book did have a happy ending.

EMILE: On what planet, dude?

RETT: It's all a matter of perspective, Emile. For example, whose good was Jon concerned about? His own or God's?

EMILE: Well…God's. But–

RETT: And whose good was advanced in the end? Jon's or God's?

EMILE: Well…God's.

RETT: Then your opinion on whether or not this book has a happy ending depends on your perspective of what is truly good and important: Our good or God's. Personally, I found myself feeling renewed after reading it.

DANE: All right, let me ask you guys a serious question. [reads from his notebook] If you could write your own story and take whatever fictional liberties you wanted, how would it be different from your life today? And how would it end?

EMILE: [raises his hand] Can I go first?

DANE: Of course, Emile. Go ahead.

EMILE: OK, first, can this be a movie? Or does it have to be like a regular book?

MARTIN: [*to* SAM] If nothing else, he's predictable.

DANE: Whatever you want, Emile. It can be a movie or a book with pictures in it.

EMILE: Can I have superpowers?

DANE: Sure.

MARTIN: Let me guess: You'll be able to eat a whole pizza in a single bite.

EMILE: No, dude. That's lame. I'd be the first Christian superhero. And I wouldn't just battle bad guys; I'd fly around helping people, too.

MARTIN: [*laughs*] I'm sorry, but the thought of you airborne is rather comical.

EMILE: Well, what superpower would you have, dude?

MARTIN: I already have one.

EMILE: Yeah? What is it?

MARTIN: I can travel in time, be anyone I want to be, anywhere on earth, without leaving my living room.

EMILE: How?

MARTIN: I read.

[EMILE *laughs heartily.*]

MARTIN: [*watches* EMILE *with curiosity*] And I can apparently make people laugh without trying.

EMILE: [*smiles as his laughter fades*] Dude, if you knew what I know, you'd think that was funny, too.

DANE: So, how would your story end, Emile?

EMILE: Oh, um…how would it end?

DANE: Yes.

EMILE: Well, I guess, I'd try and leave the world a better place, you know?

MARTIN: [*extends his hand toward* EMILE] Miss South Carolina, ladies and gentlemen. [*claps twice*]

DANE: Martin, come on. Be serious for a moment. Let Emile talk.

MARTIN: [*suppresses a grin*] Sorry.

EMILE: I was just going to say that I would use what God's given me to help people around me. And that's how everyone would remember me when I'm gone.

MARTIN: [*with reverence*] The benevolent Flying Pizza Man. God rest his soul.

EMILE: Something like that.

DANE: Thank you, Emile. Sam, you look deep in thought. How about your story?

SAM: Ah, well, I've been rolling that about for the last few minutes. And I can't think of anything different. Other than possibly helping more of God's smaller creatures. That really is my passion, you know. I do the best with the ones I treat; I only wish I could do more.

DANE: So, no real changes, then?

SAM: Well, I am rather content at the moment, so I'd hate to change that.

DANE: Fair enough. What about you, Rett?

RETT: I admit, the ending of our book did force me to consider whatever legacy I may leave behind. It's a sobering thought to see one's life in its entirety knowing there's an end to it. We should all take time to reflect on things that truly matter.

MARTIN: I can't tell if you're stalling or pontificating.

RETT: I'm simply answering the question.

MARTIN: Sam, be a friend and wake me when his sermon is over.

SAM: Yes, of course.

RETT: He's kidding, Sam. And I'm not preaching.

MARTIN: Well, then, make it personal, or admit that you're talking around the question.

DANE: [*smiles*] You really haven't said anything yet, Rett. So, come on. What would you change, and how would it end?

[*A slight pause*]

RETT: All right, well, I suppose there's the obvious. My character would still be with his family, and he'd still be a respected pastor.

DANE: Would your character have a real seminary degree or just have better luck?

RETT: If I could change one thing in my story, it would be that. I would have finished seminary and gotten my doctorate. I would have borrowed the money for tuition and just got it done. I guess I was just afraid of the debt.

[EMILE *chuckles and shakes his head.*]

RETT: [*to* EMILE] Student loan debt is a serious concern, Emile.

EMILE: Oh, I know, dude. I was just laughing at something else.

DANE: So, how would your story end, Rett?

RETT: It wouldn't matter. If I knew I was serving the Lord like he wanted me to, I'd accept whatever end he wanted to write for me.

DANE: Even if it was like Jon's in the book?

RETT: Sure. Look at his legacy. I'm assuming he was the "seed for the harvest." If my life could be used by God to help grow his kingdom after I'm gone, then whatever happens to me doesn't matter.

MARTIN: How fictionally magnanimous of you.

RETT: Well, that was the exercise, Martin: to help us see ourselves outside of our own reality and history. I'm curious about your answer.

DANE: That's right, Martin. You're next.

MARTIN: Is this sort of our final exam question for the class?

DANE: Sure. For a hundred percent of your grade.

RETT: And, like you said to me, you have to make it personal.

EMILE: Dude, it's Martin.

RETT: [*nods*] Good point.

MARTIN: All right, well…for starters, I wouldn't be an assistant librarian. My fictional Martin would have a respectable position. Something his wife could tell her friends about at parties and be proud of. And he would be a good husband. And a good father. And his phone would have so many pictures of his daughter, it would constantly be running out of space to hold them. And he would take her to Disney World…and see her off on her first date…and then to prom and off to college. And he would walk her down the aisle and give her away to someone who couldn't possibly deserve such a beautiful woman. And he would grow old with his wife and be surrounded by his grandchildren as he quietly passes away in his bed…the end. [*pauses*] Not very exciting, is it? I doubt it would sell very well. Probably end up in the free bin outside 2nd & Charles.

[DANE *and* RETT *exchange glances.*]

EMILE: Um, like, I'm not sure if this is the right time or not, but…I'd like to tell you guys where I was last week. I think it might help.

DANE: OK, Emile, go ahead.

EMILE: Well, after I told my mom about getting saved and all, here a few weeks ago, she made me go talk to her priest about it. And I was kind of nervous at first, thinking maybe he'd tell me I did something wrong, or it didn't count or something like that. But actually, he was pretty cool about it. And he asked me what I was going to do with my new faith. And I was like, what do you mean? And he said something from the Bible about how Jesus said people will know who belongs to him by how they love one another.

RETT: John 13:35.

EMILE: Yeah. And I got to thinking about this group and thought, what could I do to show how much I, you know…love you guys.

RETT: That's very nice, Emile.

EMILE: Well, wait; it gets better. So, I started trying to pray about it and then a few days later, the guy who helps me manage all my money and stuff called and said he had a unique investment opportunity for me. And I'm like, what's that? And it turns out I bought a company!

DANE: Wow. What kind of company, Emile?

EMILE: That's the really cool part. It's a publishing company! And, Dane, I've already told them I want to publish your book!

DANE: Whoa.

RETT: That's great, Emile!

DANE: But Emile…you haven't even read my manuscript.

EMILE: That's OK. My new Assistant Editor and Reader will do that for me. Won't you, Martin?

MARTIN: Huh?

EMILE: [*opens his book bag, pulls out an envelope and hands it to* MARTIN] I've got a job for you, man!

[MARTIN *opens the envelope, unfolds a letter and begins to read.*]

RETT: Emile, that's amazing!

EMILE: [*to* RETT] Hang on. I've got something for you, too, man. [*opens his book bag, pulls out an envelope and hands it to* RETT] Here.

[RETT *opens the envelope, unfolds a letter and begins to read.*]

EMILE: Read it out loud.

RETT: "We are pleased to award you the inaugural Gills Creek Five Memorial Scholarship–

EMILE: That's us! [*points to the letter*] The Gills Creek Five! Keep reading.

RETT: [*continues reading*] "contingent upon your successful application and readmission to Southwestern Baptist Theological Seminary." Emile, what is this?

EMILE: It's a full ride, man! You can be Dr. McCasguill, again. But for real, this time! And I've set it up so you get to pick a new scholarship winner every year.

[*A pause*]

RETT: [*stares at the letter in his hands*] Emile...wow.

DANE: Emile, thank you.

RETT: Yes, of course, thank you, Emile. I'm just in a bit of shock, here. My wife is going to be...I can't wait to tell her.

EMILE: This is all God's doing, man, so don't thank me.

MARTIN: I can't accept this.

EMILE: What? Of course you can, man. If the money's not right, call the lady at the bottom of the letter. And they said you can even work from home.

MARTIN: No. [*hands the letter back to* EMILE]

DANE: Why can't you accept it, Martin? It sounds perfect for you.

MARTIN: It is. But I don't deserve it. You've seen me in here over the last couple months. I've been a jerk to you, Emile. Why would you want to help me?

EMILE: Because…you're my friend, dude.

[MARTIN *huffs and shakes his head.*]

EMILE: And because I…you know…like you, man.

MARTIN: Can't bring yourself to say it, can you? That's OK. No one can.

[*A slight pause*]

RETT: Martin, do you remember what I said our first week in here?

MARTIN: Odds are I don't.

RETT: I told you it was divine providence that led you to our group, instead of the AA meeting. And looking back over the last nine weeks, I still believe that's true. God is reaching out to you Martin. He's showing his love for you. But now it's up to you to respond.

MARTIN: God doesn't love me. He's proven that in ways you don't even know about.

[*A pause*]

DANE: Martin…we know about Emma.

MARTIN: You what? How? Did Judith…?

DANE: The night you came here and passed out on the floor you told us what happened.

[*A slight pause*]

MARTIN: [*shakes his head*] I suppose divulging one's dark secrets is an occupational hazard when you drink.

DANE: Martin, I'm so sorry that happened.

MARTIN: Well, being sorry doesn't change anything. Believe me, I know. [*pauses*] I've left Judith, by the way.

DANE: You what?

MARTIN: I've been staying in a motel not far from here the last week.

DANE: But why, Martin? Why would you leave her?

MARTIN: It was inevitable. Since I've tried to stop drinking…I promised her I'd try, you know. And I have, for the most part. But without it, I just can't bear to be with her. It's just too painful.

DANE: Martin, I'm sorry.

MARTIN: So, you see, Emile, that's why I can't accept your offer. My life's a mess. I'm just a drunk living alone in a cheap motel. That's how my real story ends.

RETT: It doesn't have to, Martin.

MARTIN: Yes, it does. [*pauses*] She blames me, you know. For Emma, I mean.

RETT: Did Judith say that?

MARTIN: She doesn't have to. I can feel it whenever she looks at me. You see, I put Emma down that night in her crib. I was the last one to see her. [*pauses*] It was my job to make sure she was OK.

RETT: Martin—

MARTIN: I have a picture of her. [*reaches in his pants pocket for his phone*] Would you like to see it?

RETT: Sure.

MARTIN: [*taps his phone's screen*] There she is. [*holds his phone so* RETT *and the others can see*]

RETT: She's beautiful, Martin.

SAM: Yes, absolutely precious, Martin.

MARTIN: Thanks.

DANE: And the stuffed animal next to her…that wouldn't be….

MARTIN: That's Herman.

> [*A pause as* MARTIN *puts his phone back in his pocket*]
> [*Other members of the group look to each other as they process what they heard.*]

RETT: Martin, you've experienced something no one should ever have to go through. I can't imagine what that pain must feel like. And I know there aren't any words I can offer that will make it go away. But I know someone who can help you. Someone who knows what it's like to lose a child. Someone who can help you feel love and forgiveness and give you a new hope.

MARTIN: You're going to say God, aren't you?

RETT: Yes, Martin, I am.

[MARTIN *chuckles lightly and looks down.*]

RETT: Martin, I know deep down, he's the only reason you've been coming back here, week after week. And whether you admit it or not, he's the hope you're clinging to. The hope that there must be something more than this miserable life we find ourselves in, sometimes. The hope that someone can love us, despite all our mistakes and all our faults, and wash away the constant guilt and pain. God gives us that hope, Martin. It's in all of us. And the answer is his Son, Jesus Christ.

MARTIN: That's fine for you. And Dane and Sam and Emile. But I'm not a Believer.

RETT: It's a choice, Martin. We've all made that choice to believe. To put our faith in God's plan of salvation for us, by believing that Jesus came and died and rose again for us. You've lost a child; you know what that's like. Can you imagine going through that willingly for someone else's benefit?

MARTIN: No.

RETT: But that's what God did for you, Martin. He loves you so much that he let his only Child die for you. And all he wants in return is your love and trust.

MARTIN: But I'm afraid I've made myself quite unlovable. Judith is a living testament to that.

RETT: You said a minute ago you feel guilt and blame whenever you look into Judith's eyes. You know what I think you're seeing? You're seeing the same pain and emptiness you feel. She's hurting just like you. She needs the same love and hope that you need. And she's looking for you to give her that, Martin.

MARTIN: I don't think I have it in me.

RETT: Then let God give it to you. If you want to be a good husband, like your "fictional Martin," you need the love that comes from knowing him. And there's only one way to get that, Martin. You need Jesus.

[*A slight pause*]

MARTIN: [*grins slightly as he keeps his eyes down*] This is my chapter, isn't it?

RETT: Your chapter?

MARTIN: In our book here. [*looks at the book in his hands and fans its pages*] The assortment of characters – the doctor, the co-ed, the air conditioner repairman, the truck driver – they each get a chapter to make a decision. This is my chapter, isn't it?

RETT: If you want to look at it that way, sure. But you know, some of those characters said yes, and some said no. The question is, Martin, which choice will you make?

[*A pause*]

MARTIN: [*with a slight grin*] I suppose you'll have to wait for the sequel to find out.

RETT: [*looks to* DANE *and sighs*] I tried.

DANE: [*offers a consoling smile*] Good job, Pastor.

EMILE: Martin, if you ever want to, you know, talk about stuff, I'm always around.

MARTIN: Thank you, Emile.

EMILE: And I want you to hang on to this until next week. [*hands the offer letter back to* MARTIN] Just think about it, OK, dude?

MARTIN: [*takes the envelope*] Fair enough.

EMILE: Oh, and I've got one more thing. [*reaches into his book bag, pulls out another envelope, and hands it to* SAM]

SAM: What's this, Emile?

EMILE: Open it and you'll find out.

SAM: [*opens the envelope and scans over the letter*] I'm afraid I don't understand. This is a letter from the pet shelter expressing their gratitude. For what I'm not sure.

EMILE: You're now an official sponsor of the Fur Ball, dude! Read it.

SAM: "Palmetto Pets would like to sincerely thank Reigning Cats and Dogs Veterinary Clinic for their generous contribution to our fundraising efforts. Your gift represents over ten percent of our annual operating budget and ensures loving care and adoptions for hundreds of Palmetto pets." [*looks to* EMILE] But all I did was buy a ticket to the event.

EMILE: Sam, I had my financial guy set-up this thing called an annuity that will make quarterly donations to the shelter in your name. I was going to get you a puppy, but I thought this would be better.

SAM: Emile, this is truly wonderful. I don't know how I could ever thank you. I can't wait to share the news with my staff.

EMILE: And with Hannah.

DANE: Yeah, big date coming up this weekend, right Sam?

SAM: Oh, yes. I'm rather nervous about that.

RETT: You'll do fine, Sam.

SAM: I'll look forward to telling you all about it next week.

DANE: How 'bout we all go grab some coffee and celebrate?

EMILE: If you make it ice cream, I'll buy.

SAM: Ice cream sounds wonderful.

DANE: Ice cream it is, then.

RETT: Let's go.

[*All stand, except* MARTIN.]

DANE: You coming, Martin?

MARTIN: No, you go ahead. I'll catch-up.

DANE: OK. We'll be at the little ice cream place just down the street next to Moe's.

MARTIN: Next to Moe's. Got it. [*gives a slight wave*]

[DANE, EMILE, SAM *and* RETT *move toward the door.*]

EMILE: [*to* SAM] Dude, they have a Captain Crunch flavor!

SAM: Who's Captain Crunch?

DANE: They also have a nice French roast mocha flavor. [*winks at* RETT]

RETT: Hey, ça m'a l'air bien!

DANE: [*smiles and pats* RETT *on the back as the group exits*] I have no idea what that means.

[*The group exits, leaving* MARTIN *sitting alone. Eyes down, he sits motionless for a moment. He leans forward to rest his elbows on his knees and lets his head hang from his shoulders. After a moment, he lifts his head, wipes tears from his eyes and pulls his phone from his pocket. After turning it on, he stares at the screen. He taps his finger on the screen, holds the phone to his ear and waits.*]

MARTIN: Hey...Please don't hang up...I have something I want to tell you.

Curtain

EPILOGUE

The Lost Bean

Characters

DANE
MARTIN
SAM
HANNAH
JUDITH
JULIA

Scene

The Lost Bean coffee shop in Columbia, South Carolina

Time

Thursday night at 7:30

A medium sized coffee shop called the LOST BEAN *two years after the group's last meeting. A large rustic high-top table surrounded by eight bar stools sits in the middle of the café. To the left are an assortment of small two-top tables with chairs, none matching the other. To the right are two pairs of soft leather chairs each with a marble coffee table before them. Along the right wall is the coffee bar where guests place their orders. The main entrance to the shop is to the left of the coffee bar on the back wall. The café is half full of customers.* DANE *and* MARTIN *enter. They approach the bar and study the menu hanging above it.*

MARTIN: What do you normally get here?

DANE: I usually just get a medium roast drip coffee. Black. Sometimes a shot of espresso.

MARTIN: That's it? And you call yourself a coffee snob.

DANE: I do.

MARTIN: I expected you to order something a little more impressive than that.

DANE: Alright, let me ask you: When you were a practicing alcoholic, did you drink straight liquor, or did you order the frou-frou drinks with the umbrellas and made-up names?

MARTIN: Well…mostly straight liquor, I suppose. Or something very close to it.

DANE: So, you were an alcohol snob. Why would you expect me to be any different with coffee?

MARTIN: [*nods his head*] A solid defense, sir. I tip my hat to you.

BARISTA: Hey, Dane. We have a nice single origin roast from Brazil today you might like.

DANE: Perfect, thanks. And that's for here. And I'll get his, too. [*nods to* MARTIN]

MARTIN: [*to the* BARISTA] I'll have a glass of milk.

[DANE *laughs*]

MARTIN: What?

DANE: Milk?

MARTIN: [*to the* BARISTA] OK, make it chocolate milk. Hot. [*to* DANE] Is that better?

DANE: If you were ten years old, yes. [*pays for the order as they turn to find a table*] Are you off caffeine now, too?

MARTIN: I'm just finally comfortable facing life the way God made me. No stimulants or depressants required. [*extends his arms outward*] This was his design, so it's good enough for me.

[DANE *leads them to the large high-top table*]

DANE: Wow, suddenly I feel blasphemous for ordering a cup of coffee. Thanks, Martin.

MARTIN: My pleasure. [*takes his seat on a bar stool next to* DANE] So, did you get a hold of Emile?

DANE: I did. He's actually in Italy this week with his mom visiting the Vatican. Kind of a bucket list trip for her.

MARTIN: That's nice of him. Did she take her burrito?

DANE: [*laughs*] I didn't ask.

[*A café staff member places their drinks in front of them on the table.*]

DANE: Thank you. [*to* MARTIN] So, how's work?

MARTIN: I'm still enjoying it. To get paid for reading feels like stealing. Not that every submission is worth reading, mind you. But, still, I don't think I could ever thank Emile enough. [*takes a sip of his hot chocolate*] Incidentally, you'll never guess what crossed my desk a few months ago.

DANE: Um…Emile's first novel.

MARTIN: [*laughs*] Oh, God, could you imagine? The word count for "dude" alone would fill most books.

[DANE *laughs*]

MARTIN (CONT'): No, actually I read a manuscript written by your author from our study group a couple years ago.

DANE: Are you serious?

MARTIN: That's always a good question with me; but yes, I am serious.

DANE: What's it about? Is it good?

MARTIN: Let's see…how do I sum this up? It's about time travelers from an alternative future timeline who travel back to 1963 to assassinate JFK to prevent the nuclear holocaust which led to the post-apocalyptic mess in which they lived. How does that grab you?

DANE: Wow. That's quite a departure from his first book.

MARTIN: Actually, it's an improvement.

DANE: But didn't Stephen King already do something like that?

MARTIN: He did. And as a publishable, sellable work, that's the biggest problem we have with his manuscript. But here's the kicker: What would you say if I told you that the manuscript's author is the proud owner of the very coffee shop in which I'm now sipping this delicious hot chocolate? [*takes a sip from his cup*]

DANE: What?! Are you serious? [*looks around the café*]

MARTIN: Again, good question. And yes.

DANE: The same guy I talked to here two years ago?

MARTIN: One in the same.

DANE: Oh, man, that's crazy. [*still looking around the café*] I've seen him in here since then, but I had no reason to think he even worked here, much less owned it. He's never doing anything. Just hanging out, reading or talking to someone.

MARTIN: Well, if I owned a coffee shop, that's what I would do.

DANE: That's all you do now.

MARTIN: [*nods*] That's a fair point. [*sips his drink*]

DANE: I wish I would have known that when I talked with him a couple years ago.

MARTIN: [*grins*] So, if you could go back in time and spend ten minutes with him, what would you say?

DANE: I'd probably...oh, yeah. [*chuckles*] My question from the study group.

MARTIN: [*nods*] It comes full circle. By the way, I actually got my ten minutes.

DANE: With who? Your girlfriend from college?

MARTIN: Yep. Emma.

DANE: You wanted to know why she broke up with you, right?

MARTIN: Exactly.

DANE: You got to talk to her?

MARTIN: I did. Not in person, mind you. She followed me on Instagram last week, thinking I wouldn't know who she was. Different last name and all. But I recognized her immediately, even after all the years. So, I requested a follow back, and she accepted. [*pauses*] I have to tell you, – and I'm embarrassed to say this – but when I saw that she had accepted my request to follow her, I felt...a happiness I hadn't felt in, well, I don't know when I've ever felt like that. It was this...ten seconds of pure, silent joy. Like every atom of my being was smiling. And then it faded. And I was back to just regular Martin.

DANE: Sounds like you experienced a little endorphin high.

MARTIN: Well, it was better than alcohol, I can tell you that. Without the hangover.

DANE: So, did you message her or something?

MARTIN: I did. I sent her a note thanking her for connecting. And she replied saying she never thought in a million years I'd know who she was. As if I'd ever forget her. She apparently had no clue what state she left me in when she broke up with me. I never stopped thinking about her. Ever. [*sips his hot chocolate*] And I started to think about what it was like those months after it was over. I was hurt. I was angry. I was lost. And all of that started to come back to me. So, then I asked myself, why had I been so happy to hear from this person who had dumped me without batting an eye? It doesn't make emotional sense.

DANE: [*chuckles*] Emotions and logic don't really go together, you know.

MARTIN: No, I suppose not. But listen to this: After we exchanged a few platitudes back and forth – you know, "you look the same," "so do you" – you know what she asked me?

DANE: What?

MARTIN: She asked me why we broke up.

DANE: *She* asked *you* that?

MARTIN: Yep. Can you believe that? It's like John Wilkes Booth asking who shot Lincoln.

DANE: [*laughs*] I get your point, but that may be overstating it just a bit. [*sips his coffee*]

MARTIN: Maybe. So, you know what I told her?

DANE: I'm almost afraid to ask.

MARTIN: I told her we broke up so I could meet and marry the love of my life, Judith.

DANE: Oh, gosh. How did she take that?

MARTIN: After keeping me waiting a minute or two, she said how happy she was for me. And that was that. And you know what, for the first time since all that happened, I felt free from it. No more wondering. No more regrets. No more wishing. It was all gone.

DANE: That's quite a gift.

MARTIN: It was. And then suddenly, I couldn't wait for Judith to get home from work. I couldn't wait to see her. I cleaned the whole house and cooked us dinner and took little Dave with me to the store and bought flowers to go on the table.

DANE: I still can't believe you named your son Dave.

MARTIN: [*smiles*] After you!

DANE: Very funny. Anyway, I'm sure all your efforts made Judith happy.

MARTIN: [*sips his hot chocolate*] Well, that's not quite how it worked out.

DANE: What do you mean?

MARTIN: She had a bad day at work and came home late and exhausted. She didn't notice the house being cleaned or the flowers. She ate dinner, complained about her boss in between bites, and then got into bed.

DANE: Hmph...and how did that make you feel?

MARTIN: How did that make me feel? What are you my therapist now?

DANE: [*chuckles*] I'm sorry, I couldn't think of anything else to say.

MARTIN: Well, since empathy isn't one of your strong suits, I'll play along: It didn't bother me in the least.

DANE: Seriously? After you did all that, and she didn't even notice?

MARTIN: Dane, here's where I am with all things Judith: I love her. And I'm honored to be her husband. She's been a source of stability and strength even when I was a mess and weak. You've seen me like that, you know what a pain I was.

DANE: Well....

MARTIN: Anyway, since we've both seen the light, faith-wise, I'm just so [*pauses*] grateful, I guess is the right word.

DANE: [*smiles*] That's a great place to be.

MARTIN: It is. [*turns fully toward* DANE] Which makes me wonder, what about you?

[SAM *enters the cafe looking lost and a bit nervous as he waits to place an order.*]

DANE: [*sips his coffee*] What about me?

MARTIN: I've never heard you, even once, mention a potential love interest. You've been divorced as long as I've

185

known you, but surely you have something going on, don't you? You have to.

DANE: Why do I have to?

MARTIN: Because it's…. [*notices* SAM *looking at the menu board*] Look there's Sam; even he has a girl. Surely you see the irony in that, don't you? You, a faith-centered, well-read, not-so-old bachelor, goes on—

DANE: You forgot published author.

MARTIN: Alright, published author. Even more so. How is it that you go home alone when Sam, of all men, is happily in love with Hannah?

DANE: How do you know I don't have something going on?

MARTIN: Well, do you?

[SAM *appears at the table with a cup of tea in his hand*]

DANE: Hey, Sam.

SAM: Hello, Dane. Martin.

MARTIN: What are you drinking, there, Sam?

SAM: Ah, well, [*looks at the cup in his hand*] I know this is Dane's favorite coffee house, but I've never really had a taste for it. Coffee, that is. [*takes a seat next to* MARTIN] My mother always felt obliged to brew a pot whenever we had family visiting, but as I recall no one ever drank any of it. I've always suspected she just wanted the spent grounds for her garden. She had quite the green thumb, you know. She grew—

DANE: Sam.

SAM: Yes?

DANE: What are you drinking?

SAM: Oh, yes. Sorry. A London Fog.

MARTIN: How appropriate.

[DANE *chuckles*]

SAM: I'm sorry if I appear a bit scattered this evening. I'm just nervous, I suppose.

DANE: What's there to be nervous about Sam?

SAM: [*looks to* MARTIN] I'm not sure if I'm allowed to say. Martin?

MARTIN: You have my permission to tell him, Sam.

DANE: What's going on, guys?

SAM: Well, I–

MARTIN: Sam is taking the big leap. He's proposing to Hannah.

DANE: Wow, that's great, Sam! Congrats! When?

SAM: Here, tonight.

DANE: Here?

MARTIN: Judith and Hannah are having dinner, and Judith is bringing her here afterwards.

DANE: Does she know you'll be here, Sam?

SAM: I don't believe so. That is the plan, at least. I've relied on Martin's direction for all this.

DANE: [*looks with concern to* MARTIN] Martin, please tell me this is all above board.

MARTIN: Of course, it is. Do you really think I'd toy with little Sam, here, over something like that?

DANE: Yes.

MARTIN: Well, sorry to disappoint, but Sam and I have this all planned out. Tonight, he's going to ask the girl he loves to spend the rest of her life in riveting conversations about house pets and deworming procedures.

DANE: Well, I'm very excited for you Sam. Just relax. You're going to do great.

SAM: Maybe if we rehearsed it one more time, Martin, I might feel more prepared.

MARTIN: [*looks around*] I'm not having you drop to one knee and propose to me in the Lost Bean. Just do what we talked about, and you'll be fine.

[SAM *pulls a notepad from his pocket and stares at it intensely, his lips moving as he reads.*]

MARTIN: And for God's sake, don't pull out your notepad when she gets here.

SAM: Right, of course. [*puts his notepad away.*]

MARTIN: [*turns back to* DANE] So, anyway, back to you. Do you have something going on you'd like to tell us about?

DANE: [*sips his coffee*] Such as?

MARTIN: You know what I'm talking about. Romance, women, the good life!

DANE: I'm living a good life, Martin. I'm happy.

MARTIN: Being satisfied with low expectations is not the same as happiness.

DANE: Is that another one of your quotes?

MARTIN: No, that was mine. But you can quote me, if you like.

DANE: Next time I talk with Rett, I'll be sure and do that. He said to tell you guys "Hello," by the way.

SAM: Has he earned his degree?

DANE: Almost. His former church has offered to bring him back in some capacity when he's done. All things forgiven.

SAM: Well, I say good on Rett. A man of his caliber deserves a second chance. I certainly hope we see him again someday.

MARTIN: Um, excuse me. How did I lose the floor, here? [*to* DANE] We were in a conversation.

DANE: That's funny, it felt more like an interrogation.

MARTIN: I just find it hard to believe that you've given up on love.

DANE: Did I say I've given up?

MARTIN: You have an active disinterest in the whole subject. That's the same as giving up.

[JULIA *appears at the table with a wiping cloth in her hand.*]

JULIA: Everybody doing OK over here?

DANE: Hey, Julia. We're good, thanks.

[JULIA *returns to the bar.* SAM *pulls out his notebook and begins to read again, mouthing the words.*]

MARTIN: [*after watching* JULIA *leave*] What about Julia?

DANE: What about her?

MARTIN: Why not her? She seems nice. She smiled at you.

SAM: [*gazes toward* JULIA] And she is rather attractive.

MARTIN: Hannah, Sam. You're on in a few minutes, remember?

SAM: Oh, yes. Right. Of course.

DANE: Guys, Julia works here. I'm a regular and she works for tips. [*to* MARTIN] You know how that works, Mr. Barfly.

MARTIN: I'm not giving up on this, you know. You need something to look forward to in life.

DANE: I have things to look forward to.

MARTIN: Such as?

DANE: I–

MARTIN: And if you say drinking coffee or grading papers, I win.

DANE: [*with resignation*] Well, I guess you win, then.

MARTIN: [*sighs*] You're hopeless. [*Sees* HANNAH *and* JUDITH *enter the café*] Here come Judith and Hannah. We'll continue this later.

[HANNAH *and* JUDITH *approach the table.* HANNAH *is smiling joyfully as she rushes up next to* SAM.]

HANNAH: Hey! I didn't know you'd be here!

SAM: It's a surprise.

MARTIN: [*chuckles*] Nice, Sam.

HANNAH: Oh, my gosh! Guess what! We just saw the most romantic thing ever!

MARTIN: Hello, Martin, how are you?

HANNAH: [*quickly*] Sorry, hey, Martin. [*glowing*] It was amazing!

JUDITH: [*to* MARTIN] We had dinner at Market on Main and sat outside in that big courtyard they have with the live music and big screen TV.

HANNAH: And we saw a couple get engaged! And he sang to her!

SAM: He sang to her? [*looks at* MARTIN]

HANNAH: He did! He got the band to play that song I like called "I'll Be" by Edward McCain.

MARTIN: Edwin.

HANNAH: Who?

MARTIN: It's Edwin McCain.

HANNAH: Yeah, anyway, and he went up with the band and he sang it to her! And in the middle of the song while the band played, he waved her up and he got down on one knee and he pulled out a ring and asked her, right there!

SAM: And…she said yes?

HANNAH: Of course, she said yes! And this is the best part: You know those big fans they have outside there to cool everyone off and keep the bugs away? When she said yes, he had someone toss up rose petals in front of the fans and they came falling down on them like confetti! And then the band kept playing while they held each other and slow danced. [*closes her eyes and smiles*] It was so romantic. Just like a dream.

SAM: My…I say, [*looks to* MARTIN] that is quite the story.

MARTIN: [*to* HANNAH] You know, one could make the argument that all that was very inconsiderate on his part.

HANNAH: What? How?

MARTIN: Putting her on the spot like that in such an obviously over-produced, public manner. I think most women would prefer a more sensible, modest proposal. [*to* JUDITH] Wouldn't you agree, honey?

JUDITH: You mean like your proposal to me, Marty?

MARTIN: Well…it's not fair to use me as an example.

JUDITH: [*to everyone else*] He proposed to me on the couch in the middle of a Seinfeld episode.

DANE: [*laughs heartily*] Mr. Romance, here, did that?

JUDITH: He did.

MARTIN: Well, it was an inspiring episode.

JUDITH: [*smiles at* MARTIN] And I did say yes.

MARTIN: [*looks to* SAM] See?

SAM: I'm a bit confused.

MARTIN: I can fix that. OK, everyone, Sam has something he'd like to say. [*turns to* SAM] Go ahead, Sam.

SAM: What? *Now*, Martin? I couldn't. I….

MARTIN: [*gently*] Go ahead, Sam.

[SAM *shakes his head.* MARTIN *puts his hand on* SAM's *shoulder.*]

MARTIN: It's OK. Just do what we talked about. Trust me.

SAM: Well….

DANE: Come on, Sam. Give it a go, as you like to say.

HANNAH: [*eyes bouncing around the table*] What's going on?

SAM: Well. [*turns to* HANNAH] Hannah….

HANNAH: Yes?

SAM: We've been…. [*clears his throat*] Yes, um…. [*clears his throat*] Hannah….

HANNAH: Yes?

SAM: We've been a dating couple going on these last two years, and…there is something I'd like to say. Or ask, as it were. [*takes a deep breath*] Hannah….

HANNAH: Yes?

SAM: Well…um…how was dinner?

MARTIN: Sam.

HANNAH: It was fine.

SAM: Yes, good. Right. [*clears his throat and stiffens a bit*] Hannah….

HANNAH: Yes?

SAM: Um…John Keats once said, "I love that you believed me–

MARTIN: Nope. Try again.

SAM: Uh…"I love you the more I believe you…."

MARTIN: No, Sam, it's, "I love you the more in that I believe you… [*waves his hand encouraging* SAM *to finish the quote to no avail*] had liked me for my own sake and for nothing else."

SAM: Ah, yes. [*looks to* HANNAH] What he just said.

HANNAH: Who is John Keats?

MARTIN: Who's John Keats? Seriously?

JUDITH: Marty, let Sam talk. This is his night.

MARTIN: I would if he'd get the words right.

SAM: [to HANNAH] Let me try this again…Hannah….

HANNAH: Yes?

SAM: I love… [*takes out his notepad and opens it.*] I love…oh, buggar! [*tosses his notepad aside and drops to one knee*] Hannah, darling, I wanted all this to go so perfectly here tonight, and it's off the rails, already. I'm not one for singing, at least outside of a pub, and I don't know who Edward McCain is–

MARTIN: Edwin.

JUDITH: *Shhh.*

SAM: And I don't have any rose petals or large fans.

HANNAH: Sam, honey, what are you talking about? Judy said we were just coming here to have a piece of cheesecake.

SAM: What kind of cheesecake?

DANE: Sam, focus.

SAM: Yes, um…Hannah.

HANNAH: Yes?

SAM: I love you, and I believe you love me, just the way I am. And that makes me so happy.

MARTIN: [*smiling*] That sums up Keats, nicely.

JUDITH: *Shhh!*

SAM: [*takes* HANNAH's *hand*] Hannah....

HANNAH: Yes?

SAM: I would be honored to have you as my wife. [*pulls a ring from his pocket and holds it up to her*] Will you marry me?

HANNAH: [*smiles softly*] Yes.

SAM: I promise to take good care of you and Major Tom, who by the way will get a family discount once we're married.

HANNAH: [*laughs*] Yes, Sam.

SAM: I know I'm a bit wanting in the field of romance, but I–

JUDITH: Sam, stop talking. She said yes.

SAM: Yes? [*to* HANNAH] You said, yes?

HANNAH: Yes, Sam. It's all I ever wanted.

[SAM *stands and embraces* HANNAH, *while those watching around the cafe applaud.* JUDITH *and* HANNAH *embrace.* DANE *and* MARTIN *pat* SAM *on the back and shake* SAM's *hand*]

MARTIN: Congrats, my friend.

SAM: Thank you, Martin. I couldn't have done it without you.

MARTIN: You almost didn't do it *with* me. But that was all you in the end. Good job.

[JUDITH *pulls* MARTIN *aside and talks to him privately.*]

DANE: Best wishes to you, Sam. I couldn't be happier for you and Hannah.

SAM: Thank you, Dane. This all started with your group, you know. I'm eternally grateful to you. I can't imagine my life these last two years without you and Martin and Emile.

DANE: I know Emile will be excited for you when he finds out. And Rett, too.

SAM: Yes, I'm sorry they couldn't be here.

[MARTIN *returns to* SAM *and* DANE]

MARTIN: Alright, the girls want to go get ice cream to celebrate. You in Dane?

DANE: No, I've got some coffee to finish and papers to grade here. [*winks at* MARTIN]

MARTIN: Very funny.

SAM: Are you sure, Dane? You'll be missed.

DANE: No, you go ahead, Sam. Sounds like more of a couples-thing anyway.

MARTIN: Well, we're going to fix that, soon. You're next, you know.

DANE: Whatever you say, Martin. You're the matchmaker.

[MARTIN, JUDITH, SAM *and* HANNAH *say their goodbyes to* DANE *and leave.* DANE *sits alone at the table tinkering with the pieces of a chess board.* JULIA *approaches.*]

JULIA: Got time for another game?

DANE: [*smiles*] I do, if you do.

JULIA: This place can live without me for a little while.

DANE: History teacher by day, barista by night. I don't know how you do it.

JULIA: How else would I get to play you in chess?

[DANE *chuckles as he sets up the board.*]

JULIA (CONT'): I should warn you, though. I've been studying chess strategy. I'm going to own you one day.

DANE: [*smiles warmly*] I'm looking forward to it.

Curtain

ABOUT THE AUTHOR

A native of South Carolina, Greg is a former IT professional and coffee shop owner. His four novels have received a total of fourteen independent publishing book awards and honors. Having crafted relatable, realistic, and sometimes humorous character-driven stories in the Christian fiction genre with *A Seed for the Harvest* (2014) and *The Gills Creek Five* (2017), Greg explores coming-of-age themes in a 1974 summer beach setting in *The Sea Turtle* (2023). His latest award-winning novel, *The Ballad of Walker Owens* (2024), is available in paperback, hardcover, Kindle, and Apple Books editions. While each of Greg's novels are unique in style and story, the savvy reader will note they share the same story universe.

Greg earned both his bachelor's and master's degrees from the University of South Carolina and lives in Columbia, SC with his wife and two dogs.

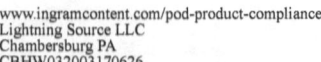